I0578808

Time Exposure

CLICK DUET – BOOK TWO

PERSEPHONE AUTUMN

BETWEEN WORDS PUBLISHING LLC

Time Exposure

Copyright © 2021 by Persephone Autumn

www.persephoneautumn.com

All rights reserved.

No part of this book may be reproduced in any form or by any electronic or mechanical means, including photocopying, information storage and retrieval systems, without written permission from the author except for the use of brief quotations in a book review.

This book is a work of fiction. Names, characters, establishments, organizations, and incidents are either products of the author's imagination or are used fictitiously to give a sense of authenticity. Any resemblance to actual events, places, or persons, living or dead, is entirely coincidental.

If you're reading this book and did not purchase it, or it was not purchased for your use only, or it was purchased on a site I do not advertise I sell on, then it was pirated illegally. Please purchase a copy of your own on a platform where the author advertises she distributes and respect the hard work of this author.

ISBN: 978-1-951477-14-1 (Ebook)

ISBN: 978-1-951477-15-8 (Paperback)

Editor: Ellie McLove | My Brother's Editor

Proofreader: Rosa Sharon | My Brother's Editor

Cover Design: Kat Savage | Kat Savage Designs

Books by Persephone Autumn

Bay Area Duet Series

Click Duet

Through the Lens

Time Exposure

Inked Duet

Fine Line

Love Buzz

Insomniac Duet

Restless Night

A Love So Bright

Artist Duet

Blank Canvas

Abstract Passion

Devotion Series

Distorted Devotion

Undying Devotion

Beloved Devotion

Darkest Devotion

Standalone Romance Novels

Depths Awakened

Sweet Tooth

Transcendental

Poetry Collections

Ink Veins

Broken Metronome

Slipping From Existence

Standalone Horror Novels

By Dawn (published under P. Autumn)

To those who looked challenge in the face and said, "You don't choose my fate. I do."

Time Exposure

Photography term.

Exposure is the total amount of light that hits the sensor for one frame or shot. It is determined by the exposure triangle settings (ISO, aperture and shutter speed).

How much light is captured depends on three things: aperture size in the lens, ISO sensitivity on your camera's sensor, and the length of *time* you leave the shutter open.

"Like I said, I'm Layla. Gavin's fiancée."

Fuck, fuck, fuck…

Why the hell is she doing this? What does Layla stand to gain by doing this? By ruining the one chance I have at getting Cora back. What did Alyson offer her in return?

Cora's eyes grow impossibly wide as her soft green irises darken and tears pool in the corners. Her jaw drops as she stands stoic, eyes bouncing between me and Layla. For a moment, she doesn't move a muscle or utter a single word. And her stillness scares the shit out of me.

When her synapsis fire again, Cora takes a few cautious steps forward, bends over and picks her shoes up from the floor. I stand helpless, less than five feet away, and observe her as she squats down to sit on the floor and slides the sneakers on. Her movements are slow and measured. She makes it a point to make zero eye contact with me as she ties her laces with precision. The longer she keeps her head down, focusing on the task, the less I breathe.

Every moment we shared over the last week just nose-dived off my balcony. Every word I said, every promise I made, she will now perceive as a lie. After all this time, after everything we have endured, our second chance at forever will be ruined at the hands of two petty, jealous, greedy bitches.

But not if I get a say in the matter.

I rip my arm from Layla's grip and jerk away from her. Heat and anger boil my blood and explode from my pores as I turn to face Layla. "Fucking leave. Now!" My voice is venomous and louder than she expects and she startles. Her momentary wide eyes twitch before she yanks on her bitter bitch mask.

"What the fuck, Gavin?" Layla bites back. "You don't want your *soul mate* to know about us?" The way she rolls soul mate over her tongue is dangerous. Poisonous. Vile.

What the fuck is Layla's deal? She has never been like this. Never stepped up and blocked me from what I want. Acting like a jealous girlfriend. Or a straight-up bitch. This is a whole new side and it disgusts me.

"There is no *us*," I snap. "Your need for attention has no bounds, does it? Get the fuck away from me. Your little arrangement… done. I'm done."

I shove Layla out the door and her eyes widen once more before I slam the door in her face. Not sure what provoked her to act vindictively, but as soon as I fix things with Cora, I will settle things with Layla.

Bitch.

I walk over to where Cora sits on the floor and hesitantly kneel in front of her. Lowering my head, I try to get her to look up at me. Her head hangs low as her eyes hone in on her shoes. Slowly, she loops and ties them, but doesn't peek up. I desperately want to reach forward, slip my fingers under her chin and tip her head back so she will look at me. But I don't. Because it scares the shit out of me to see what is in her eyes right now.

"Cora? Baby? Look at me," I whisper. My voice is gruff and dry, and I don't recognize the pitch with my own ears.

Her chin pops up and her eyes snap to mine. "Don't you dare," she seethes as she scoots away from me with a finger pointed at my face.

"What?" I ask, confused. "Don't what, baby?" This won't be good, but I need her to tell me what she is thinking. What she is feeling. Because fuck, I am scared shitless.

Cora unsteadily rises to her feet and locks eyes with me as I stand. I take a step in her direction and she steps back before lifting her hands to stop me. Tears well in her eyes. Her exposed skin painted in red blotchy patterns. Eyes narrow and straighten over and over as she assesses me. Pain etches the lines of her forehead as her chin starts to quiver.

And fuck if I am not losing my goddamn mind because she won't let me get any closer to her. Won't let me touch her. Won't let me connect with and soothe her. The once-old stab wound in my heart slices wide open and the pain of this whole situation lances me.

I cannot lose her. Not again.

"Don't call me *baby*." My term of endearment for her spits out like acid on her tongue. "Not after some woman you've never mentioned tells me she's your fiancée. What the actual fuck, Gavin?" With each word Cora speaks, her volume goes from soft to livid in a matter of seconds.

Cora isn't just angry with me or this situation, she is fucking furious. Can't say I blame her, but I wish there was an abbreviated way to explain it. One where she would understand. One where the nightmare we are currently stuck in will transition into your average dream.

Unfortunately, this nightmare is very real. And it won't go away with the blink of an eye.

Just out of arm's reach, her frame shakes as she clenches her fists so tight her knuckles whiten. Her jaw tightens as she stares at me and subtly shakes her head. Eyes glassy, but the tears have yet to spill down her cheeks.

I take another step forward and she steps back again.

Each step she takes away from me is a knife twisting my heart. Raw and painful and a reminder of the suffering we both endured thirteen years ago. A pain neither of us will survive again.

Holding my hands up in surrender, I gaze into her wet, red eyes. "Baby," I say, cringing when she grinds her teeth. "Please, let me explain. It's not what you think. Layla is just a friend. We aren't actually engaged."

Cora cocks her head and glares at me, unbelieving. Her eyes lock on mine and study them as if I just asked her to read my palm. She scrutinizes them a moment before eyeing the lines of my face and finally dropping to stare at my lips. I know what she is doing. Because Cora and I don't have to speak for reality to be stated. So, instead of asking me more questions, she tries to read the truth through my expressions and body language.

And god I hope she sees the truth in my words. Because they are nothing but real.

Layla has never been anything other than a friend. Our relationship has never skirted any line other than friendship. And Layla stating she is my fiancée… there is more to the story than meets the eye. A story privy to me, Layla, and Alyson. A story I hope Cora gives me a chance to explain.

Just when I spot a glimmer of hope, Cora speaks. And her words are far from what I expect to come out of her mouth.

"This can't happen, Gavin." She gestures between

us. "This is too much. Even if you are telling me the truth now, I can't deal with bullshit drama like this. Women claiming ownership over you. Women saying vicious things to steal you from me. Why would you hide something like this from me? Because you thought it would never be an issue between us?" She pauses to catch her breath. "I knew this was a mistake. I need to leave."

No. No, no, no. This cannot be happening. This cannot be fucking happening. I cannot lose her. Not again. And not over this.

She swipes her purse from the table and starts for the door. I freeze momentarily, not wanting to believe this is my reality. That I am losing her again after finally getting her back. It's like I am sixteen all over again. Like I don't have a say in the matter. Like what I want doesn't count and won't be taken into consideration.

I refuse to let this be how we end. Downright refuse.

The heavy hotel room door slams shut and snaps me back to reality. *No!*

I bolt to the door and yank it open. Stepping out into the hall, I look left then right before spotting Cora. She isn't running, but her feet trek along the carpet faster than a steady walk. I sprint after her, giving no fucks that I have just locked myself out of my room.

"Cora," I yell. "Wait. Please, let me fix this."

She stands in front of the elevator banks and religiously mashes the down button like her life depends on it. Her teary eyes glance my way and it rips open every suture in my stitched-up heart.

I did this to her. I hurt her. Again.

The elevator car arrives and she steps in, the doors closing just as I approach. *Damnit.* I smash the down button, hopeful the elevator car she stepped in reopens. Seconds later, the other set of doors opens and I jump in and hit the button for the bottom floor. The car pings as it passes each floor, my heart wrenching tighter and tighter with each second I spend away from her. Not knowing if she has already reached the lobby and is darting out the doors to her car.

When the doors slide open, I dash out and scan the lobby for Cora. My eyes land on her as she weaves between people in the full reception area and I race toward her. As long as she remains in my line of sight, I will catch her. I will not let her go this easily. Not after the strides we have made this week. Not after I got back the only person who matters.

"Cora," I yell. Instantly, every set of eyes on the ground floor whips my way. "Please wait."

She peers over her shoulder, tears trailing down her cheeks, and makes a beeline for the exit. Just as she makes it to the door, I catch up to her and grab hold of her arm. As badly as I want to haul her into me, to wrap my arms around her and pin her to my chest, I stop myself. Now is not the time. Although I won't let her leave without a fight, I won't be the man who doesn't give her a choice. After everything we have endured, she deserves to choose what happens next.

"Let me go, Gavin," she spits out as she tries to yank her arm from my grasp.

"No, baby. Please, let's talk about this," I beg. "Please let me explain everything. I wasn't intentionally keeping this from you. And, like I said, it's not real."

Her soft, sad bloodshot eyes stare up at me, pleading with me to let her go as nonstop tears spill down her cheeks.

This pain, her pain… what she is experiencing in this very moment. If it is even remotely close to what she felt when I left thirteen years ago, I hate myself. I hate myself for doing this to her. For letting her experience such heartbreaking emotions. Again. No one should have to undergo this form of torture—once, let alone twice.

"Please, Gavin," she mumbles, her eyes darting around the room. Embarrassment creases her brow as she squeezes her eyes shut. "Please just let me go." When she opens her eyes, a new emotion paints her expression. Disparity and numbness. An emptiness that has me stumbling back, physically and mentally. "Can't you see?"

See what? That I have inflicted the worst pain on the sole person I live and breathe for. Yes, I see it. I hate that I see it. But something twists in my gut and stabs at my heart. And I have a feeling her words have an ulterior meaning. Definition unbeknownst to me.

"See what, baby?" I ask, terrified to know the answer. Terrified of what she will say next.

I ache to touch her. Yearn to embrace her and pepper kisses on her hair, her temples, her forehead. But I fear the worst. That she will pull away. Reject me. And her rejection would sting worse than any words. So, I keep my hands at my sides and imagine all the ways I wish to right my wrongs.

"Isn't it obvious?" she asks, not waiting for me to answer before she continues. "It's like the universe is trying to tell us something."

Cocking my head, I narrow my eyes in confusion. Is she suggesting what I think she is? That we don't belong together. That as much as we love each other, we aren't meant to have each other.

How could something so perfect not be meant to exist?

The universe isn't trying to tell us shit. And if for some nonsensical reason she believes fate is telling us we don't belong together; I will grab fate by the balls until it comprehends the truth. That Cora and I belong together. Always have and always will.

And until I fix this, nothing else matters.

"Baby, I have no idea what you're thinking, but it better not be anything along the lines that we aren't meant to be together. Because that's bullshit and you know it."

Cora turns away from me and walks out the exit with

me hot on her heels. Her pace picks up and I jog to keep up with her. She darts past the valet and heads for the lot where she parked her car.

I will not suffocate her. She needs time to mull things over. But she has to know things between us won't get better if we don't discuss them. She needs to hear the whole story.

When she reaches her car, her hands dive in her purse and shove stuff left to right as she searches for her keys. She pulls out the fob and unlocks her car as I jog up to her.

"Baby, please don't leave. Let's go back up to my room and talk about this." We need to talk, that is the only way to resolve this.

"No, Gavin. As much as I want this, as much as I want us to be together, it feels like the world is against us. And I can't do it. I can't fight anymore. I fought for so many years. Cried a million tears until my eyes couldn't do it anymore. And it's happening all over again. My heart fell in love with you all over again and I let it. *Stupid, stupid girl.* As soon as I allowed myself to be vulnerable, I got crushed. I feel like the earth is swallowing me whole, like it's clawing at my insides and eating me alive. And I can't deal with it. Can't deal with you. Not now."

Her words paralyze me. Make my limbs numb and my heart hollow. Pain spills out of her and infiltrates me like liquid poison. Slithers in my veins and takes up residence. And it doesn't just hurt. It kills.

The first time we were separated, it was against what I wanted. Against what either of us wanted. But I had no say or power to stop my parents from moving us across the country for my mom's promotion. Although I was older, I was still just a child.

Now, I may no longer be a child, but I inflict her with the same heartache and torture. Except this time around, our emotional state has evolved. We understand love and hope and pain and anguish. We grasp fear and hopelessness and sorrow and dejection. And in the blink of an hour, I have given all of them to her.

I have never hated myself as much as I do right now.

I step into her, a tear slipping down my cheek as she steps back and bumps into her car. But I ignore her retreat and reach up, framing her face in my hands. This will not be the last time I see her; I won't let it be. This is not how our story ends.

"I fucked up, and I'm so sorry. So, so sorry. But I will fix this. I swear to you, I will fix this. And when I do, I'm coming back for you. You can count on it. Because, Cora" —I pause, pinching my eyes shut— "you and I belong together. No matter what obstacles come at us, we belong together. I love you. And I will always love you. Until my last breath. Until my dying day."

I lean down, press my lips to hers and kiss her softly.

Our tears blend at our joined lips and I don't know which are hers and which are mine. When I break the kiss, I lick our tears from my lips and step away. She stares at me a second as hundreds of thoughts invade her mind. Then she rushes to get in her car, starts the engine and drives away.

Away from me. Away from us.

I will give her time, but I won't go down without a fight. Not this time. Never again.

I can't breathe. Literally.

A block from Gavin's hotel, I turn onto a small side street and shift my car into park. The engine idles quietly as I rest my forehead against the steering wheel. Tears flood my eyes and blur the world around me. Violent sobs wrack my body as I lose all sense of composure. With every breath I try to inhale, the emotional boulder in my throat grows larger and heavier.

He said it isn't real. That this supposed engagement is a farce. A fallacy. Said *she* is only a friend. Just a friend. Nothing more. But if all of what he said is true, why do I feel like this? Empty. Broken. Shattered. Desolate.

Why do I feel as if I have just lost the one person who makes me whole? The one person who soothes the ache. Makes me smile. Mends the wounds once created from his loss. A loss he had zero control over.

I replay snippets of the conversation in my head, trying to find truth in Gavin's words. Trying to *listen* to what he said. Really listen. Because the moment she announced their supposed relationship, the world spun off its axis. I wobbled. Stumbled backward in time. Back to a time when vows were made. To the day he left and promised to return, but abandoned me for more than a decade.

He swears he and this other woman are not in a relationship. That he and this other woman are not betrothed. That they are just friends. Only friends. But why would Gavin's friend say such things? Cruel words meant to inflict pain. To make me suffer.

As is, my memory is one huge blob of confusion right now. It mixes in words and visuals from various conversations. Mingles them like partygoers. And I hate it. Hate that I don't know what is real and what is artifice. I have no way of knowing what memory is fact or fable.

So how can I decipher what to believe and what to disregard? And how the hell will I handle what happens next? I just don't know. Can't think past what just happened or the laceration in my heart.

The one thing I do know with absolute certainty is I cannot sit on this beach another minute, crying my eyes out. Sooner or later, a cop will tell me to move along. Tell me I cannot be parked here because I don't have a permit. Who cares if I cry so hard I risk an accident. Who cares if I have a meltdown and can't feel my limbs.

And with that, another round of sobs takes hold. I let it out, fishing a napkin from my glove compartment to blow my nose and dry some of the tears. When my cries slightly settle and I can breathe a little, I decide going home isn't the best option.

I grab my purse from the passenger seat and dig out my cell phone. With shaky hands, I unlock the phone and call Shelly. The ringing blares in my ear while I attempt to stop crying altogether. On the third ring, Shelly answers.

"Hey, girl. How's it going?" Shelly cajoles.

I don't answer right away as I still work to control my tears and breathing. But it is no use and I start blubbering like a baby. The semi-composed state I was in moments ago vanishes.

"Cora?" she beckons, panic edging her voice. "Cora, are you okay? What's wrong?"

"I… I'm… Shelly…" I fumble, my words a mess of inconsistency. Just like my head. Just like my heart. "Shelly, can I… can I come over?" I manage to frame the question around my sobs.

"Oh my god! Are you okay, Cora? What's happening?"

She still hasn't answered my question. *Please just tell me to come over. Just tell me it is okay.* Not that I really need an invitation to her house, but I don't want to intrude if she has plans.

"Shelly, please. Please can I come over?" I plead

through my incessant tears and sobs. I wish the blubbering would just stop. It hurts. Every muscle and bone and organ just hurts.

"Yes, of course you can. Are you okay to drive? I can pick you up."

As tempting as her offer is, if I leave my car on the beach it will get impounded. And that is a whole separate nightmare I don't need. Bad enough my heart is in shambles, I don't need to have automobile and financial issues too. Shelly lives in a small one-bedroom in Largo, and I should be able to make it there in twenty minutes. If I collect myself mentally, driving to her house shouldn't be an issue. It won't take long. Then I can let it all go again.

"You don't need to come and get me. I'm leaving Clearwater Beach. Should be there in twenty to thirty, depending on the traffic."

"Cora, you've got me worried. Did something happen? Are you okay? Is Gavin okay?"

Just hearing his name brings about a new bout of tears. My chest caves in on itself as my heart shrivels and lungs forget how to function. *Breathe Cora.*

"I'll tell you when I get to your house. See you soon."

And before she can say or ask anything else, I disconnect the call. If I plan to make it to her house in one piece, I need to clear my head as much as possible. Her infinite questions won't help matters. She can ask them all when I get to her place.

I sit unmoving in the car another couple minutes, taking deep breaths and attempting to refocus on physical objects.

A man walks his dog on the sidewalk. The neon signs across the street promote beer and pizza and a live band. A child swings wildly between her parents as they head into a seafood restaurant. *Breathe in. Breathe out. Just remember to breathe, Cora.* The flash of the pedestrian crossing sign lights up. An older woman rides by on a tricycle with colorful lights.

Once calm enough to drive, I turn the car around, drive off the beach and head in the direction of Shelly's place.

A couple blocks down, I crank up the radio and play loud, upbeat music. Then I roll down the windows and let the wind pelt my skin and whip my hair. Minutes later, I no longer smell the salty beach air and am hit with the occasional scent of fast food or well water. But right now, I would rather smell the foul odor of greasy meat and sulfur than the beach.

Because no matter how much time passes, the sight, smell and feel of the beach will always remind me of Gavin. Always.

After weaving down a couple streets, I park my car in front of Shelly's apartment building. As I get out of the car, I spot Shelly running down the stairs and heading in my direction. She slams into me and wraps her arms around me, squeezing me with boa constrictor strength.

And I don't pry her off me. I simply cry into her shoulder. Soaking her hair and shirt. Couldn't tell you if anyone passed by us. I honestly don't give a damn.

We stand like this for a while before she breaks the hug. "Come on, let's go inside."

I don't say a word, stumbling beside her with my arm hooked in hers. She guides us inside, takes my keys and purse and sets them on the coffee table. We plop down on the couch and she hugs me close again, stroking my hair. She lets me cry and sob until my body can no longer do either anymore. Shelly knows exactly what I need and doesn't bother trying to ask more questions. Not yet, anyway.

When my sobs recede, Shelly assumes I have reached the max quota for tears in one day. She leans away from me and ducks her head to look me in the eyes. "You want to talk about it?"

And for the first time since I arrived, our eyes finally meet and hold. Her expression a heaping pile of concern as she regards me. My eyes feel ten times bigger than normal and sting from crying for the last hour straight. No doubt they are bloodshot and lifeless.

Lifeless. Exactly how I feel right now.

"It's Gavin," I say as I stare at my fumbling hands in my lap. If I look back up and see sadness in Shelly's eyes, I will lose it again. And I am so tired of crying. So very tired. It hurts too fucking much.

Shelly rubs my back with gentle, endearing strokes. "What about Gavin?"

I swallow, not wanting to speak about the fiasco that happened tonight, but knowing full well I need to get it off my chest. To tell someone. To get insight from someone I trust.

Gavin told me none of it was true. That they were only friends. But if they were only friends and not actually engaged, why would he hide all of it from me? He never mentioned her as being one of his friends. Or a fellow model. Actually, he hasn't mentioned anyone he knows in California aside from his mom. And something about that doesn't sit well with me.

Does he not want me to know about his life the last thirteen years? Does he have something to hide?

Inhaling deeply, I prepare to recant the evening before I called. *Deep breaths, Cora. You need to let it all out.*

"Gavin and I went back to his hotel after spending the day together. He invited me up to his room and I obliged. Everything was good. Perfect, actually. We cuddled on the couch and started watching Netflix. Halfway through the show, someone knocked on the door. We were both confused by it, but Gavin said it was probably someone at the wrong room and he'd send them away."

I stop talking. Stare at my fumbling fingers in my lap. Pick at a loose thread along the hem of my shirt. Bite the inside of my cheek and try my best not to start crying. Again.

If what Gavin said was true, why is this so hard to say? Why is it so hard for me to believe? To believe he is telling me nothing except the truth. Once upon a time, I never doubted a single word Gavin spoke. So, why do I doubt him now?

And although the answer lingers at the edge of my thoughts, I don't dare voice it. Not now. Not yet.

"Take your time, Cora. Do you want some water?"

I nod as I wring my shirt between my hands. She returns seconds later and hands me a glass. I drink the water and thank her. After I place the glass on the table, I rip the bandage from the wound in my chest and continue.

"When Gavin didn't come right back to the couch, I wondered who was at the door and what was taking so long. I headed for the door and heard him arguing with a woman. At first, I couldn't make out what they were saying, but could tell they knew each other. For a moment, I thought maybe it was his agent. When I was close enough to hear them talking, I heard Gavin tell the woman he was planning to move back to Florida. At that point, I knew it wasn't his agent because they'd already discussed him moving back. The woman seemed pissed and asked what was so great about being here. Just as she asked him, she caught sight of me."

Shelly gasps and slaps a hand over her mouth as her

eyes widen. And suddenly, it seems I don't need to tell her what happens next, because she already knows. She may not know the pertinent details, but she has a vague idea. And I plan to tell her everything. To get it all off my chest. I need to. Because bottling this up will kill me.

"The second her eyes landed on me; an evil smile lit up her face. Like she knew who I was. Like what would happen next would hurt me and Gavin, but she didn't give a shit. Anyway, after she saw me, she became sweet and formal. She introduced herself—"

"What's her name?" Shelly interrupts.

"Layla."

For a minute, Shelly lifts her eyes to the ceiling and studies the popcorn as if it is art. She searches her memory bank for anyone with the name Layla. But her search will yield no results. Because if Gavin didn't mention her to me, I am positive he didn't mention her to anyone else. Not even Micah. Why would he?

"Don't know her," Shelly confirms.

"Me either. She's one of his California friends. After she introduced herself, she asked who I was. Seconds after, Gavin tried to make her leave. More than once. But she was insistent on staying and butting in. After no one spoke for a moment, she smiled big again and tells me she's Gavin's fiancée."

Shelly's jaw drops to the floor as she stares at me. As her mouth closes, she narrows her eyes. "I'm sorry, what? I must have misheard you. Did you just say this bitch is his fiancée?"

I nod as a fresh round of tears escapes and spills down my cheeks. "But he swears it's not true. He wanted to *explain* it to me, but I bolted. And after he chased me down the hall and through the lobby and to my car, I didn't want to hear any of it. Because even if what he says is true, why didn't he tell me? We've talked so much over the last week. So why not explain it to me then? Why hide something like this if it means nothing?"

And that is the biggest question of them all. If what Gavin told me is correct—that he and Layla are not together—why not tell me about her from the get-go? If there is nothing to hide, he should have been forthcoming. Not let me find out later or in some roundabout way.

Shelly nods as she sits immobile. Her eyes fog over as her brain works double time. I stare at her as she sorts through all the details and tries to devise possible reasons why Gavin left this one piece of information out. Layla isn't some minor tidbit. Not equivalent to admitting you have a dog that may not get along with my cat. No, Layla is a huge bomb to leave unattended. A bomb that blew up in both our faces.

As it stands right now, my heart feels like it has been run over by a semitruck. Then it backed up and squashed me a second time for good measure. My head hurts—from the endless tears I keep crying and the thought that Gavin lied to me. Yes, it was a lie of omission. But he could have just told me and purposely chose not to.

And that hurts more than anything.

With his line of thinking, I have no doubt he planned to fly back to California and cut ties with whatever "fake engagement" he and this Layla woman have. Then, I would be none the wiser. Right? But I am a firm believer in the old adage "everything happens for a reason." There is a reason Gavin never brought her up. Perhaps he thought it would be pointless. Maybe he thought the two of us would never meet and didn't see why it was pertinent to disclose that part of his past. Or maybe he couldn't figure out a way to tell me without hurting me. I have no clue. The only question rolling around in my head now is why did I need to know? What do I gain from this?

Do I only want to know because it is a piece of Gavin? A part of his past that doesn't include me. A gap filled by another person. Another woman. A woman who he claims is just a friend after she flaunted their familiarity.

Is this me punishing myself? Pushing him away so he doesn't break my heart again? Although, fragments are chipping from the edges and falling to my feet.

"I don't want you driving home tonight," Shelly says as she sweeps a few stray hairs from my face and tucks them behind my ear.

And the last thing I want tonight is to be alone. Shelly probably knows this—twenty-plus years of friendship teaches you these things. Plus, going home would entail me stripping the sheets from my bed. Sheets that smell of Gavin and me and the two of us tangled together this morning. Sheets full of memories of his lips on mine, his hands on my skin, his body fit perfectly against mine.

"You're okay with me staying?"

"As if you have to ask." She leans forward and wraps her arms around me. "You are always welcome in my home. No matter what."

I hug her as if it was our last. Shelly is a great friend. The best a girl could ask for. And I am thankful every day I have her in my life. To have her big heart and warm hugs.

After the couch transitions to my makeshift bed for the night, Shelly gives me one last hug before going to her room. I turn off the tall floor lamp across the room and slip under the blanket. The moment my eyes close, flashes of Gavin spill from my memory.

Memories of us as teenagers—at school, under our tree, walking the beach at sunset, our first kiss—and memories of the last week—his cocksure smile, how easily we slipped back into old habits, the way he *looked* at me, how he held me, kissed me, promised me the future.

And I am crippled by the pain that spins a vicious web throughout my body. It twists and spirals and weaves itself around my organs and engulfs me with an unfamiliar force. The gravity of it all crushes my heart ten times more aggressively than it did thirteen years ago. Knocks the breath from my lungs. Blinds me.

I draw my knees to my chest and wrap my arms around them as another wave of tears bleeds from my eyes. As my body tremors more violent than the earth ever could.

How could I let this happen again? How could I get in this deep? Let myself fall in love with Gavin Hunt a second time?

The answer is simple. Always has been. I belong to Gavin. But does he belong to me?

Thirteen years ago

THE PLANE JOLTS forward as the wheels touch down. A shriek from the brakes echoes in my ears and I wince. I stare out the window and take in the landscape surrounding the airport as we taxi to our gate. I haven't stepped off the plane yet and I already hate this place. Hate everything it represents. Hate everything it stole from me.

I reach around to my back pocket and grab my phone. After switching off airplane mode, I open the text screen and type out a message to Cora.

Gavin: Just landed. It's only been hours, but I miss you already. So much.

My phone jingles and pings with notifications as it catches up from being offline the last six hours. Seconds later, Cora responds. Her notification the only one I check.

Cora: I miss you too. Text or call when you get to your new house.

House is the operative word in her message. Because where my parents are moving us to is a house. Not a home. There is only one place I will ever call home. Wherever Cora is. She will always be my home.

Gavin: I will. Hopefully we'll get there soon.

"Let's go, Gavin." Dad nudges me and tilts his head toward the plane's exit.

I swipe my backpack from under the seat in front of me and shuffle out of the cramped seating. Once we deplane, I hang ten feet back from my parents. Let the throng of people separate us on occasion. Although my mom's promotion is a good thing for her career and our family, I am beyond irritated with this whole situation. The only way to express my anger and frustration is to ignore them.

Is my logic juvenile? Yes. Do I give a fuck? No.

As we walk through the airport, Mom and Dad take turns peering over their shoulder every other minute.

They have concerns, I get it. But where the hell am I going to go? Not like I can jump on a plane and leave. I have no clue where I am. Nor do I know anyone here. All my friends live in Florida. Every part of my life exists on the opposite side of the country. The one person that matters most, the one I left my heart with, is thousands of miles from here.

I grind my teeth so hard my jaw aches. The thought of making new friends sends a fresh wave of irritation through my veins. Feels as if I am entering kindergarten all over again. The new kid. In the middle of high school. Just before the school year ends.

Complete and utter bullshit.

We reach the baggage claim and wait like fish for bait. The metal carousel circles around a continuous loop. I lean against a far wall and watch as my parents patiently wait for our two pieces of luggage. Normally, I would wait beside them. Offer to help. But seeing as I hate this whole situation, I choose to stand here and go through my notifications.

Micah sent a text while we were in the air.

Micah: Let me know when you land bro. Can't believe you're gone. Who am I going to do stupid shit with now?

I type out a quick reply to him and tap send.

Gavin: Right? At least you know other people there. I'm a loner here. Fucking hate it.

My parents step up to me, but I keep my eyes on my phone as if unaware. How long can I avoid eye contact with them? At this rate, weeks seem probable. If I piss them off enough, would they let me go back to Florida? Maybe, but I highly doubt it. Micah's parents would probably let me stay with them if we asked nice enough.

"Gavin, we're leaving. Put your phone away. You can text your friends later," Mom snaps.

Is she pissed at me? Good. Maybe a dose of her own medicine will do her some good. Because pissed is all I have felt since she told me we were moving to this shithole. Since the moment she told me I didn't have a choice—or voice—in the matter. She didn't even give me a chance to protest. Her word was the final say.

Fucking bullshit.

I follow in my parents' wake as we exit the airport and my Dad hails a cab. After our luggage is crammed into the trunk, I slide in front beside the driver rather than sit with one of my parents. I have no animosity with Dad, but it seems only fair I treat them equally. After all, they are a team. And they made this decision together. Without me. Without taking any part of my life into account.

We drive away from the airport and I lean against the window, staring at nothing. I don't care if this place holds good qualities. Mountains or celebrities or monuments. None of it matters. Because I don't want to be here. An hour later, the cabbie parks in "our driveway." He helps Dad get the luggage from the trunk before driving away a minute later.

I stay rooted at the end of the driveway and stare at the house I will never call home. A desert-colored Spanish-style house with vines growing up one side of the exterior. Large, grassy plants rest along the front edges of the structure; red rocks fill in the plant bed. The grass mowed with perfect precision. Sporadic large windows fill the walls with the occasional extended half-round window. A small iron gate encloses the driveway from the house to the set-back garage.

Nothing about this house resembles the home we left behind in Florida. This place feels like something to flaunt. A dollar sign. A pretentious badge of honor. Nothing about it could ever be homey. The core of it too frigid and formal. Too "look at me and the salary increase I just earned."

My stomach roils at the idea of my family becoming snotty or ostentatious. Of throwing black-tie parties and drinking with our pinkies out and tilting our noses higher.

When did my parents become these people?

Several minutes pass before I decide to go inside. My parents nowhere in sight when I enter. No doubt they are wandering the property and making sure there is no damage. I scan the bare interior, the moving truck not arriving until the day after tomorrow. *Fucking bullshit.* We have to sleep on the damn floor until our shit arrives. Could we not even get air mattresses?

I walk down a hall and find the room Mom said would be mine. Once inside, I shut the door and lay on the tan carpet. No matter how many photos or posters I add to the walls, this room will never be mine. At most, I will only live here the next two years and then fly back to Florida. Back to Cora and Micah and everything I love.

I crawl over to the suitcase deposited in my room— probably by Dad. Unzipping the case, I riffle through the contents until I locate what I search for. Tucked between my jeans is a small wooden box. I trace my fingertips over the lightly stained grain, a tear slipping from my eye as I stare at my most prized possession. My favorite birthday present from my favorite person.

The box is about the size of a novel, but deeper. Cora used a wood burning tool and inscribed our names on the top surface as well as the date when we became official. Then she got artsy and added a beach sunset.

I brush my fingers over our names and the tears spill heavier. Not even a full day has passed and I can't breathe. The constant warmth I once felt beneath my sternum is now cold and sunken and empty. Without Cora nearby, the world wobbles off-kilter. Revolves slower. Shifts to an endless night.

Flipping the small latch, I open the box and stare at

the contents. Lose focus as the one person who means more to me than anyone else is just a memory in a fucking box. One by one, I pull each item from the box. One by one, I cry a little more. So many photos. Of us together—laughing, kissing, watching television. Of Cora by herself—some posed, some candid. Goofy faces, serious faces, expressions she reserved only for me. Drawings she did on napkins, scrap pieces of paper and other random types of paper. Some folded, some small enough to sit open in the box. Most she doesn't even know I possess. Small tokens of her I kept since the day we met.

Pieces of her. Pieces of *us*.

I set the drawings on the fluffy carpet and spread them out so I have an unobstructed view of them all at the same time. Once I have them all spread, I go back to the box and take out the next items. Photos.

Polaroids and regular four-by-six printed images. Cora almost always had a camera with her everywhere we went. She kept it stashed in her purse or backpack, taking it out whenever an opportunity presented itself. Most of the photos on her camera—an older, thirty-five-millimeter film Nikon—were of places, things or other people. Every once in a while, I would snatch her camera and shoot pictures of her. And every once in a while, we were able to get someone else to take a photo of us together.

Sifting through the photos, I land on one of my two

favorites. The photo is just of Cora. We were wandering along the trail in Walsingham Park and I had been holding her camera for a bit after she stopped to use the restroom. At the time, I had been walking ten feet behind her. Her eyes drifted up to the trees, searching for birds or squirrels. Or maybe she was simply admiring the trees—she did that sometimes, got lost staring at the trees. I lifted the camera to my eye and snapped the shutter, capturing her profile with the sunbeams haloing around her. She looked like a peaceful angel. My peaceful angel.

When she printed the black and whites, she teased me and asked why I took the picture. My response to her was "you just looked so peaceful and in your element. I wanted to capture the moment." All she did was nod and smile.

My second favorite photo was of the two of us. More like our silhouettes. In the photo, we stood side by side with an arm around each other. A friendly guy on the beach snapped the photo as the sun set behind us. It wasn't noticeable to most people who glanced at the photo, but we were both smiling like idiots. Giddy after dating each other for six months. Just looking at the photo now makes me smile like a fool. A fool madly in love with his soul mate.

I set the two photos beside each other and stare at them a while. Go back to the time they were taken. Remember how I felt those days. How the sight of her made my heart swell and breath vanish. Tears drip from my chin and splatter on the photos. I trace my finger over Cora in each of the pictures.

Fuck. Two years away from Cora will feel like an eternity.

"Gavin?" Mom bellows from somewhere outside the four walls that will now be my room.

I ignore her call a minute as I continue going through the box. Get lost in the drawings and photos as tears continue to fall. But the moment doesn't last long.

Knock, knock, knock.

"Gavin, didn't you hear me calling you?" Mom asks. In my periphery, she stands in the doorway with her hands on her hips, staring at my profile and the scattered images.

After a moment, I lift my tear-stained eyes to hers. *Yeah, I heard you. But I don't fucking care.* That is what I want to say to her. But I don't. Instead, I lie.

"Nope."

I don't elaborate. Don't give her anything to expand on. Because I don't want to look at her. Don't want to speak to her. And a second later, I go back to staring at the items in front of me. But she interrupts me again and I groan.

"Well, Dad and I were thinking we should go out and grab something to eat. Maybe see what's near here too. Sound good?"

She is doing her best in a shitty situation she is aware upsets me. And I guess I should reciprocate and try not to be too much of a dick. I mean, is it really such a bad thing that she is good at what she does? That her boss deemed her better than others in her field. A good son would be happy for his mom. A good son would be proud. But every time I try to be happy for her, all I think about is how I drew the short end of the stick in this whole situation. How I had no say or alternative.

I may be sixteen, but shouldn't my voice count in matters like this? Shouldn't I have a say?

"Yeah, Mom. Can you give me a few minutes? I want to call Cora before it's too late for her."

Something new to deal with. Fucking time zone differences. Bad enough I don't get to see her or speak to her regularly. Now I have to fight with the fact that our lives exist with a three-hour time disruption.

"Sure thing. Ten minutes. And then we'll go."

"Thanks, Mom."

She gives me a sad smile then closes my door and walks off. Once she has been gone a few seconds, I call Cora.

She answers on the first ring. The moment I hear her voice, every live wire inside of me calms. Almost three thousand miles away and Cora still holds the balm to my heart. We talk nonstop for ten minutes—her more than me. She talks about Shelly hanging out with her and staying over at her house. How they have been watching *Lord of the Rings* on repeat and Shelly wants to kill her. This makes me laugh for the first time in weeks.

And then Cora becomes quiet. So quiet I wonder if

she fell asleep. I close my eyes for a minute and picture her sleeping with me curled up behind her. Our bodies flush and my arms wrapped around her waist. Before I ask if she is still awake, she whispers into the phone.

"It hasn't even been a whole day and I already miss you so much." Her voice trembles over the line and I know she is holding back tears. I won't tell her, but I saw her collapse outside my house as we drove away. She may have thought we were far enough away, but we weren't. And the sight of her on the ground crying crushed me. The fact I couldn't turn the car around and go to her, scoop her up in my arms and rock her to soothe the pain, kills me.

"Me too, baby."

"I'm getting a job soon. Save up money so I can fly out to see you. Maybe by our anniversary."

Hope filters through her words and spreads from her phone to mine. With it, I sense her warmth and a hint of gladness. Maybe that's what I should do too. Find a job and save money. Teens don't make much money, but earning something is better than nothing at all. Maybe I will call it my Cora fund. Both of us can save up to fly back and forth.

"That's a good idea. I'll do that too."

Just as Cora starts talking again, Dad walks into the room and signals it is time to go. I nod and hold up a finger. He taps his watch and walks out, leaving the door open. Door open equals time is up.

"Gavin?"

"I'm still here, baby. Mom and Dad said I need to get off the phone. We're going out to dinner."

"Okay." Her voice drops so low I barely hear her. And I wouldn't be surprised if the second we hang up, she starts crying all over again. I will too. Because this situation is annoying and heartbreaking and fucked up. And I hate that I can't hold her right now. Can't press her against my chest and rub a hand up and down her back. Can't promise her everything will be alright. Although, the prospect of getting a job and saving to see her again lights a fire inside me.

"I wish I didn't have to."

"I know. I love you."

"I love you, too. I'll call you in the morning."

Seconds later, and with much reluctance, the call ends. As sad and frustrated as I am with being stuck in a situation I can't reverse, hope flares anew for us. And we both hold on to that hope with every breath we take. Because hope is all we have.

But little do we know, things don't always go according to plan. And life has a way of throwing curve-balls. Curveballs that batter and bruise hearts.

Present

Something jabs me in the ribs as I roll from my side onto my back. I swipe my hand behind me in an attempt to remove said object. I pat and swipe and wave my arm. Whatever it is, it's still there. What the hell? I dig near my ribs and after no success locating the source, I flop over, land on my back and groan. Not only am I being stabbed by some invisible foreign object, but my body is on fire.

I open my eyes and squint, feeling disoriented for a moment.

Never-ending blue, puffy white clouds and the morning sun brighten the sky directly above. In my left periphery is a tall oak tree, the limbs hang overhead while the leaves flutter in the slight breeze. To my right is a row of bushy grass plants. The smell of grass and earth and something floral hits my nose. Birds chirp all around. Squirrels scamper past me. And I swear I hear ducks quacking nearby.

When I roll to sit up, every muscle in my body reacts. My back stiff, neck throbbing, shoulders sore, eyes swollen. Like I partied all night and missed all the good parts.

Once I reorient myself and attempt to work the pain from my muscles, I squint at my surroundings. Adjust to the brightness and focus on what is in front of me. Gray siding, black trim and window treatments, and bushy shrubs.

Cora's house. More accurate—Cora's back patio.

I glance over to the driveway and notice her car is still missing. And the fact that she hasn't been at home all night worries me in more ways than one. She was so upset when she left my side last night. She tried to fight it, but I could tell the dam was about to burst the second she left. I only hope wherever she is, she arrived safe.

If anything happened to her, if she got into a car wreck, I would never forgive myself. Wouldn't be able to live with myself.

"Fuck…" I mutter as I stretch my neck and back.

I walk over to the stoop by her back door and make myself comfortable. There is no way I am leaving until I know she is home and she is safe. Even if that means I sit here for hours. She may not want to talk to me right now, which I completely understand, but I won't let her run away from this. From us.

Not when I just got her back. Not after all the strides we have made. The rekindling we have done. The love I saw in her eyes when she looked into mine. I refuse to lose her.

No matter what it takes, I will fight for her. For me. For us. No chance in hell I am letting this slip through the cracks. And although it took me far too long to come back to her—and under the wrong circumstances—I won't throw in the towel now. Not happening. I won't let her give up so easily either. Our lives may be in different places now, but one fact remains one-hundred-percent unchanged.

We love each other. Plain and simple.

And nothing or no one will steal the love we share from us. Never again.

I pull my phone from my pocket—again—and check the time. Ten thirty-five. Not only have I been awake and sitting by Cora's back door for over two hours, I have been at her house for close to twelve hours. And she hasn't.

Luna is probably freaking out inside looking for her Mom and her breakfast.

Slowly but surely, I start to freak out a bit too. By now, I thought she would be home. The fact that she isn't, has me worrying more—about where she is and why she hasn't come home. Elbows resting on my knees, I drop my head in my hands and groan. *Please let her be okay.* Not in some hospital getting treated for injuries because she couldn't focus enough to drive.

But another thought crosses my mind. A thought that boils my blood and chills me to the bone simultaneously.

Who is she with? After our argument last night, would she go running into another man's arms? And not just any man, but a man she trusts. A man she is comfortable with and confides in. *Jonas.*

Would she go to him to be consoled? Would she use her friendship with him to punish me? God, I hope not. The Cora I know doesn't seem the type to do such petty or callous things. But the Cora I know isn't the Cora that exists today. And that scrap of knowledge stings more than anything.

Even if Cora refuses to see it, it is more than obvious Jonas likes her. Hell, any man who looks at a woman the way he looks at Cora doesn't just want to be friends. He may even love her.

At the thought, my skin prickles. He could be soothing her right now. Wiping her tears away. Holding her in his arms. Shushing her cries over another man. A man who claims to love her, but supposedly has a fiancée. A fake fiancée.

And suddenly it feels as if I just handed over the love of my life to another man. "What the fuck was I thinking?"

I wasn't thinking. That much is now obvious. My reaction to a friend's unfortunate situation was simple. Or so I thought at the time. My friend needed help and I offered up my solution. To make people believe we were engaged. An easy, straightforward way to improve her life. No big deal, right?

Wrong. Evidently.

But it isn't real. And Layla damn well knows nothing about our engagement is tangible. There will never be a wedding or vows or permanency. No flowers or additional jewelry or change of name.

So why the show? Why the hell did she act like a catty bitch last night? I saw the wicked gleam in her eye, the vicious curl of her lip. Why did she intentionally try to hurt the one person who matters most to me? I don't get it. Don't understand her motive. What does Layla stand to gain by ruining what Cora and I have? If Layla really was my friend, if she really cared about me as a person, she would have cheered me on. Not shattered my dreams.

So many questions need answering, but they will have to wait until later. Right now, I need to focus on fixing my relationship with Cora. It will take time to mend our relationship, but she needs to know the truth. From my lips. A truth I should have told her from the get-go.

Once I fly back to California, circumstances will change. Life will change. And unfortunately for those in my line of fire, the people stepping on my toes with stiletto heels, they will wish they never fucked me over.

It is one thing to fuck with me, individually. But it is a whole new ball game when you involve people I love.

My internal tirade gets disrupted when I hear a car pull into Cora's driveway. When I lift my head from my hands, I catch her profile behind the tint. But she is so focused on parking the car, I don't think she has spotted me yet. Not like most people survey their house the second they get home.

So, I choose to stay seated on the stoop and let her see me when she is ready.

My eyes remain glued on her as she opens the car door and steps out. As she swipes her fingers under her eyes and sniffles. As she steps around the front of her car and starts for her back door. Her eyes swollen and red. Cheeks blotchy and wet. Hair windblown. Clothes the same she wore last night. Posture defeated. And the second she notices me on her back stoop, I catch the break in her stride as she stumbles a little and takes a step back.

"Gavin?" she asks as if it is impossible for me to be

here. Her voice gruff and scratchy and parched. "What are you doing here?"

I rise, roll my neck and shoulders, and take a few tentative steps toward her. But when I do, she steps back again and keeps the distance between us. There may be ten feet between us, but it feels like ten miles. And she wants this distance because I hurt her. Again.

"Hey, baby. I was worried about you after you left last night. You were so upset. A little after you left, I got a ride here to make sure you were okay. When I saw your car wasn't here, I worried. So I stayed, wanting to be here when you got home. I needed to know you were safe and knew you wouldn't answer if I called or texted. And at some point, I must've fallen asleep."

We stand there and stare at each other. She doesn't say a word while I study her more in-depth. Her eyes are bloodshot, her green irises more opaque. Dark half-moons paint the pale skin below her dark lashes. Lines crease her forehead and the small space just above her nose pinches her brows together. She bites the inside of her cheek as she looks everywhere but at me. The blotchy patches on her cheeks spread down her neck and onto her chest.

It has only been one night and she already looks like she hasn't slept for weeks. And I am the sole reason. If she looks like this now—after just one night—how will she look for the several days I am gone? How did she look for the *years* I was gone?

A red hot poker scalds my heart at the pain I have caused her. The pain evident in her eyes and her posture and the way she reacts to me. How she purposely backs away when I try to get close. When I try to repair the shifting fault lines in her heart.

But I refuse to let everything we have gained get thrown aside like last week's leftovers. Our relationship isn't garbage and neither is how we feel about each other. Last night's debacle with Layla was just another rift. But we will get past this. We will flourish. Together.

"Gavin, I think you need to leave."

"Baby, please—"

"No," she yells. "You don't get to call me that anymore. You don't get to be smooth and sweet and all *baby* this or *baby* that. Not after what just happened. It's time for you to leave. I'm exhausted and Luna is probably crying for me. So, please. Just. Go."

"If you'd just let me explain—"

"No, Gavin. The time for explanations has passed. You should've told me about her a week ago when we were catching each other up on life. I haven't withheld anything pertinent from you. And I'd thought you'd done the same. But I guess that's what I get for thinking." She stops for a moment, chest heaving and fists clenched at her sides. When she speaks again, her voice drops and I have to fight to hear what she says. "So, *please*, I beg of you. Please leave."

I don't want to stand out here and argue with her.

Cause a scene and have her neighbors come check to see if she is okay. If anything, I want to walk her inside and wrap her in my arms and tell her everything will be okay. That I will fix the problem I created. That I will right my wrongs. And that I will return to her again.

But actions speak louder than words. And right now, she needs actions. Actions that tell her I won't break my promises. Not again. Actions that prove Layla is what I say she is. That she is a friend I did a favor for and nothing else.

I take a step toward her, and this time she doesn't back away. Her frame wilts like a sad flower, I know it's due to hurt and sleep deprivation. When I stand an arm's length from her, I reach for her hand. She doesn't stop me, but closes her eyes and hangs her head in defeat. She is tired and hurt and needs time to think. But I need her to not give up. Not on me and not on us.

Taking advantage of her non-retreat, I hold her hand for a beat. "Baby," I whisper. "I know you're upset with me. I would be, too. But I promise you, I will make this right. You and me—I am not giving up. It's not my style. Never has been. My initial reason for returning may have been for work, but once I laid eyes on you again… it was as if I could finally breathe for the first time in thirteen years. As if I became whole again. I screwed up. Big. I own this mistake. Am punishing myself for it. But when I fly back to Cali tomorrow, they won't know what hit them." With my other hand, I lift her chin so her swollen eyes meet mine. "Once I've fixed my mistakes there, I will be back. And then, I will fix what I've messed up here."

Her chin trembles in my grip. She tucks her lips between her teeth to keep from breaking down in front of me. Tears pool in her eyes as they dart between mine. She wants to believe me—I see a tinge of hope just beneath the surface—but doesn't know if she can. When all is said and done, I will be the man she deserves. The man she can believe and count on. No matter what.

"I love you, baby," I choke out as a tear rolls down my cheek. Because I won't leave here without her knowing how I feel. We may have only reconnected a week ago, but I have loved Cora half of my life. No use in denying it. "And I will be home soon. Before my birthday."

And before I can stop myself, I lean forward and place a tender kiss on her lips. Our lips may touch for less than two breaths, but those two breaths are equivalent to forever. And as difficult as it is, I back away and drop my hands from her. I grant her the space she needs.

Without another word, I step around her and walk toward the park across from her house. But just before I get out of earshot, I overhear her wails as they bounce off the trees and wisp away in the wind. Her cries for us. And for herself. And the love that binds us together like nothing else. A love that brought us together, shredded us, and will unite us again.

The second my feet touch the grassy park property, tears stream down my face. I stare back at the house briefly, and although I cannot see her, I *feel* her. Feel her anguish. And I vow to never be the reason she cries like that again. Vow to wipe away all her pain.

ONCE I MAKE IT INSIDE, I throw my purse to the floor and go feed Luna. From the back door to her food bowl, she weaves between my legs and meows her love for me. At least I have someone who will give me her undying love. All she wants in return is the occasional scoop of food, water, a clean litterbox and my affection.

If only human relationships were so simple.

I scoop Luna some food and pet her a few times while she eats and purrs simultaneously. Once she is sated, I head to the bathroom and do my business. A moment later, I swap out my clothes for a tank top and undies then crawl into my bed. Since I left the door cracked for Luna, I fetch my eye mask from my night-stand and block out any semblance of daylight.

Even if it's just a few hours, I need some sleep. Because no matter how much I tried to fall asleep on

Shelly's comfy couch, it never happened. My mind ran vicious circles in the dark. And the muffled tears never let up.

One moment, my mind was trying to rationalize the reasons he would be in a fake relationship with someone. Why he would let the world think they were engaged. What would Gavin gain from a setup like that? Especially if he professes to love me the way he does. But instead of coming up with viable answers, all I did was cry more. And I prayed that Shelly couldn't hear me sobbing into the pillow.

A few minutes later, Luna jumps onto the bed and curls up beside me. Her purrs soothe in a way nothing else does. As if she senses my forlorn demeanor, she inches her way up to my shoulder and nestles in the crook of my neck, purring stronger. I tug the sheet higher and get hit with Gavin's smell on the cotton. Upset as I am, his beachy-pine scent soothes me. Settles my soul. And within minutes, I fall asleep.

I jolt awake to the sound of my phone ringing. As badly as I want to ignore it, I can't. It could be someone other than Gavin calling me. When you work for yourself, you never get a day off.

Rolling over, I slap my hand over the surface of my bedside table until I come into contact with my phone. Not removing my eye cover, I manage to answer the call. "Hello?" My voice is raspier than a grizzly bear.

"Cora, it's Mom. Did I wake you, sweetie?"

I push the mask up to my forehead and hold the phone away from my ear a second, checking the time. *Holy shit.* It's just after three in the afternoon. I am more than thankful for the sleep, but most of the day has withered away. But it's not as if I had plans, so whatever.

"Yeah, but it's okay Mom. Is everything alright?"

A second later, a knock raps at my back door. I bolt upright and hold my breath as my heart hammers a vicious rhythm in my chest. *Shit.* Did Gavin come back? Please, please, please don't let that be him. I don't think I can deal with him—or us—right now. I just need more time to process everything.

I shove the covers from my legs and plant my feet on the floor, reluctant to move. The knock comes again as I pad down the small hall to the back door. Unfortunately for me, the back door is solid and I'm unable to see who stands on the other side—unlike my front door. I really should invest in a peephole or one of those video doorbells for the back.

As I stand at the door, hand on the knob, reluctant to turn it, my mom speaks up. "Cora, it's me. I'm the one knocking on your door."

Relief hits and I remember how to breathe again when I discover Gavin isn't the person outside my house. In the last two minutes, I somehow forgot I'd been holding the phone to my ear and my mom was on the other end. Probably because the moment there was a knock at the door, Mom stopped speaking. If she would have just told me it was her outside, I wouldn't be tiptoeing through my own house and she'd be inside already.

I twist the knob and swing the door open. I shield my eyes as the bright afternoon sun temporarily blinds me.

Stepping off to the side, I let Mom pass and then shut the door. I follow her into the kitchen and notice she's putting food in my fridge. "What's all that?" I ask.

"I stopped at the Patch and picked up a few things for you. Figured you wouldn't be in the mood to go anywhere." Her tone casual and body language easygoing. As if today is just another day.

She pulls out a couple pans and pots and starts chopping vegetables on the cutting board. Then she fills a pot with water and turns on a burner. I follow her movements for a few minutes while she busies herself in my kitchen. She moves as if she has cooked here hundreds of times, when it is quite the opposite. Of the countless times Mom has been in my home, never once has she cooked here. So watching her right now is peculiar. It isn't an anomaly to see my mom in the kitchen. But to see her in *my* kitchen, bustling around like she cooks here every day, is weird.

"Mom?"

Lifting her eyes from the cutting board, she peeks up at me. "Yeah, sweetie."

"What made you think I might not be in the mood to go anywhere?"

I have a sneaking suspicion what the answer is, but I need to know for certain before making assumptions. Before opening my mouth and spilling all the juicy details of my wretched love life.

"When Shelly came into the shop this morning, she looked a bit rough. I asked her why and she said you were at her apartment last night. She said you were upset, but didn't tell me why."

And thankfully Mom isn't one to pry, but I have no doubt she wants to know why her twenty-nine-year-old daughter spent the night at her friend's house. Pretty sure she also wants to know the source behind why I was so upset. Because why would a grown woman, who owns her own home and lives alone, go to her friend's place and spend the night? Adult friends don't generally have sleepovers on purpose.

Does Mom know Gavin is in town? Mom was friends with Gavin's mother, but I have no idea if they have kept in touch. Does she know that he was the model I photographed all week? It wouldn't be surprising if Shelly told her everything, but maybe my best friend kept this news to herself. Shelly picks and chooses what to share with Mom. She doesn't want to be the gossip mill, but she also wants to look out for me.

"Yeah, it was a rough night," I say.

Mom nods then throws noodles in the boiling water before heating up the other pan. Once the pan is hot, she adds the chopped veggies to the pan and tosses them. And right now, I love Mom more than ever.

Shelly may not have told her the reason why I am upset, but she must have indicated it was pretty bad. And what did my mom do? She left work early and went to the store, buying me groceries and comfort foods. And now, she stands in my kitchen and cooks me stir-fry. She may not know the extent of what has me upset, but she knows I need her comfort more than anything.

When the pasta finishes, she scoops it out of the water and adds it to the veggies. Then she pours in a sweetened soy sauce from my fridge. After it all comes together, she portions us both out a plateful and we go to the couch.

A few bites into the delicious meal, Mom speaks up. "So, you want to talk about it?"

She doesn't make it uncomfortable. And when I glance up from my plate, she's digging around in her plate with her chopsticks. Mom has always had a finesse with conversations. Something I never had. Not with anyone except Gavin. And even that was questionable over the last week.

Conversations with Mom have never been awkward —not even the period and sex talks when I was younger. She always has this gentleness about her. One which could console the most anxious soul. And right now, her tranquility is the exact balm I need.

Thinking back, the past week had been great. Or so I

thought. Until *she* showed up last night. Until some "fake" relationship they had was used as a weapon against me. The smile she threw after she spotted me in the room, that was nothing short of malicious. She knew her words would hurt me. Hurt us. And she tossed them like landmines and waited for the fallout.

Without further ado, the tears start back up and I immediately hate my stupid emotions and bodily functions. Can I not cry for a few non-sleeping hours? Is that too much to ask?

After I get my tear ducts under control, I peek up at my mom. "How much do you know about this past week? Besides me telling you I had a photo shoot on the beach."

She sets her plate on the table, half her food forgotten. "Shelly said Gavin was your model for the shoot."

I nod. "Did she say anything else?"

"Only that she was worried about you. But she gave me no specifics."

I set my plate beside hers, mine hardly touched. Eating is the last thing I want to do, but I appreciate that Mom isn't pushing the topic. For a moment, I stare at the fireplace as flashes of the past week flicker through my mind. Next thing, I cover my face with my hands and start crying. If Gavin leaving thirteen years ago is any indication of what is to come, I may as well just throw in the towel. Trying to be "okay" is getting old. And I am so tired of pretending to be something I am not.

Normal. Happy. Thrilled with my life.

"I let him in again, Mom. I let him wiggle his way into my heart and he broke it all over again." I stop, unable to contain the torrent spilling from my eyes.

Mom leans into me and wraps her arms around me. She shushes me while she strokes my hair and murmurs unheard words into my ear. Her hand runs slow circuits up and down my back, soothing me like only a mother can. The occasional kiss to my crown as she squeezes me closer. The extra squeeze in her hug every once in a while.

"I've got you, sweetie. No matter what, I've got you."

I sniffle between sobs. "Thanks, Mom. I love you so much."

"I love you, too. And if you want to talk about it more, I'm here. Okay?"

I squeeze her tighter and nod into her neck. "Maybe another day. I just need a day without tears."

When I told Mom I needed a day without tears, I didn't mean today. I had already cried thousands of tears today and was okay shedding more.

But shortly after Mom left, Shelly called. As if the two

of them were playing telephone tag and I was the name they passed back and forth. Shelly told me she was bringing Erin and Jonas over tonight. That we would watch movies and eat junk food and just hang out together.

The first thing I wanted to tell her was not to come over. That I wanted more alone time. Honestly, the only thing I want to do is sleep. Sleep for days or weeks or months. Sleep an eternity and erase all the bad memories. I just want everything that happened to fade away. Out of my mind. Out of my heart. Gavin. Layla. The whole thing. I want it all gone. Forgotten.

But there is no chance in hell Shelly will ever let that happen. She is determined to keep me from drowning. To keep my head above water as I gasp for breath. For life.

And that would be why my living room resembles something from our preteen years—blankets and pillows and snacks strewn across the floor. The television plays some movie from Netflix. To be honest, I have no clue what we are watching. Since the movie started, my eyes have been glazed over. My mind in a fog.

All four of us lay on the floor. Shelly on my left, Erin on her other side, and Jonas on my right. The only source of light spills from the screen. Occasionally, the room goes dark. I relish those scenes the most. The ones that give me a semblance of solitude. A breath of privacy.

Currently, Shelly's fingers play with my hair as her

eyes remain glued to the television. Erin is out of my line of sight, but I assume she's focused on the movie. And although my eyes aren't absorbing a single minute of the movie, I am fully aware that Jonas has been staring at me for the last five minutes.

And I don't know how that makes me feel.

I glance over at him—to confirm—and catch him before he can look away. His eyes crinkle at the corners and his sadness for me weighs heavier than I can bear. When he turns back to the movie, he scoots down and lays flatter. And something inside me flips. Begs for his comfort.

Shelly and Erin bring me solace, but it isn't the same. Women experience emotion different than men. They also console in other ways.

I roll onto my side and snuggle against Jonas's frame. Without hesitation, he wraps his arm around me and draws me closer. His heat warming my cool skin. But the second he places a kiss on the crown of my head, I lose it. The flood gates open once again and I cry into his shirt. Soak the cotton. With each round of tears, he holds me tighter, strokes my hair softer, shushes my cries more, and I clench his shirt in my fists harder.

We lay like this for hours—me curled into his side and him cradling me. The first movie ends and a new movie starts right after. I have no idea what plays, nor do I care. I just want to lay here and cry my eyes out. Cry until I have no more tears. Cry until I pass out.

After my tears subside a while, I sit up and notice Erin and Shelly fell asleep at some point. I envy how peaceful they both look. And I pray to whatever power resides over me, *please let me sleep tonight*. I need a deep, dreamless sleep. Just one solid night.

Jonas sits up and tenderly tucks my hair behind my ears. I don't doubt I look a hot mess right now. Hair a rat's nest. Pajamas still on from earlier when Mom was here. Eyes puffy and bloodshot. Lips cracked. But the way Jonas stares at me right now, I feel the exact opposite. His swirly blue-hazels are gentle as he searches my face.

"You want to go lay down? Maybe try to get some sleep? I'll tuck you in."

God, I hate myself and the fact I was never able to be anything but friends with Jonas. He is such a good man. A family man. Is someone I depend on. Someone I trust. Someone I care about. He likes me on a much deeper level than friendship. In the back of my mind, I think I have always been privy to this. I just shoved it away. Smothered it. Because my stupid brain has never been able to let go of Gavin.

But after everything that has happened, maybe I should let myself try again. Let myself find love with someone else. Someone who won't abandon me. Someone who will do anything for me.

"Yeah, okay," I say.

Jonas stands and extends his hand out to me. I take it

and rise from the floor. He walks me toward my bedroom with his arm around my shoulders. A sudden nervousness hits me when we walk into my bedroom. It's like nothing I have experienced with Jonas. Like a hurricane swirls beneath my ribcage.

I slip under my covers and he slides them up to my chin before sitting beside me on the bed. He gazes at me with an expression very un-Jonas. His forehead bunches and straightens and bunches again. When he reaches forward and brushes his knuckles across my cheek, the gentle touch trips a live wire inside me. I lean into his touch and close my eyes momentarily. The pent-up emotions I have ignored with Jonas detonate with ferocity.

I study his blue-rimmed hazels as they hone in on my lips. His eyes perplexed and loaded with indecision. Then his tongue darts out and wets his lips. Adam's apple bobs in his throat. But after a second, I catch a slight shake of his head. The indiscernible gesture prob- ably wasn't meant to be seen, but I am the body language detector and pick up on the smallest of signals.

"How are you?" Jonas asks, voice soft and endearing. And something tells me that wasn't what he wanted to say. But I shove the thought aside.

When most people ask me this question, I tell them I am fine. That everything is okay, although I silently scream in my head. Although I am slowly shattering inside. But there are a select few people I am straightforward with, Jonas being one of them. Shelly, Erin, and my mom being the others. I talk with Dad, but we discuss different stuff—less of the emotional, more of the rest.

"I don't know. Feels like I'm falling apart. Like someone took a chisel and hammer to my heart and started chipping it away all over again. It took so long to somewhat heal from the first time. Jonas, I don't think I'll survive this time." As the final words slip from my lips, tears roll down the sides of my face and spill to the pillow.

Jonas scoots closer, gently plants his hands on either side of my face, and leans over me. He hovers there a moment, inches from my face. From my lips. "You will get through this, Cora. I won't let it be any other way." He lifts one hand from the bed, brushes my hair from my face, and wipes away my tears. His calloused fingers so tender on my temples. "This time will not be the same," he says, huskily.

"How can you be so sure?" I ask, needing some form of reassurance.

"Because you have me and Shelly and Erin and so many others. We're all here for you. On your team. And no matter what happens, we'll be here for you."

I nod, not knowing how else to respond. But the truth in his words erases some of the chill in my bones.

"Try to get some sleep. If you need me, I'll be on the couch. And we'll all be here when you wake up in the morning."

Jonas leans in and I hold my breath as he presses his lips to my forehead. His lips are soft and warm. I close my eyes and allow myself to feel something other than sadness for a brief moment in time. To envision what life could be like if I gave Jonas a chance. If I set my heart free from the cage it has been in for far too long. Because life with Jonas would be good. Filled with smiles and laughter and warmth and love. I don't have to experience it to know it.

When he slowly lifts his lips from my skin, I shift below him and move my lips closer to his. And for a split second, our lips touch. The air crackles and steals my breath. But as quickly as our lips make contact, he breaks away.

"No, Cora." He rears back and scoots farther away from me, his eyes closed and head shaking.

Rejection hits me with incomparable force. Tears sting the backs of my eyes as I press a hand to my lips.

He doesn't want me? How could I be so stupid? What the hell was I thinking?

"I'm sorry. I just thought…" I stumble over my own words as I fight crying in front of him.

When he opens his eyes, glassy hazels stare back at me. "Please don't apologize. Believe me, I have wanted this—us—for so long. But after seeing you around Gavin this past week, it's quite clear where your heart lies. He hurt you, but you wouldn't be this devastated if you didn't still love him."

"I don't love—"

Jonas holds up his hand to stop me. "You're upset right now, and I understand why you're saying that. But you can't run from the truth, Cora. And as much as I care about you, I don't want to be the runner-up. For a long time, I thought I had a chance. But after seeing you two together, and seeing how devastated you are right now… you never fell out of love with him. And that's okay. If us just being friends is the only way I get to have you in my life, so be it. At least I get to have you."

Jonas said he cares about me. That he would be with me, if I could give him my whole heart. Although he didn't outright say he loves me, part of me deep down knows he does. But our love isn't the type to stop time. The type that consumes every breath and thought and cell. And that's okay. Because at least I still have him. Even if it isn't the way he wants. And that speaks volumes to the type of man he is.

I nod. "Okay. Thank you."

His brow knits in the middle as he tilts his head. "Why are you thanking me?"

"Because I'm so lucky to have you in my life. Lucky I met you. Our friendship is like none I've had." I swallow past the emotional lump in my throat and blink back tears. "I wouldn't get through this without you. Wouldn't make it out of this whole without you. You will always have a special place in my heart. Always."

"I know." He leans forward and kisses my cheek, his

lips lingering a little longer than friendship warrants before he sits back up. "Ditto. Try to get some sleep. And in the morning, we'll all go out to breakfast."

And before I respond, Jonas gets up and walks out of my bedroom, closing the door behind him. I don't know what I did to deserve a man like Jonas in my life, but I am indebted to whatever power brought us together. Maybe the universe knew I needed someone as tender-hearted as Jonas to help heal my heart. Not completely, but enough to live in the world.

I roll over and hug the other pillow to my chest, catching Gavin's scent. I inhale deeply and, for the first time in twenty-four hours, allow myself to purposely think about Gavin. Flutters echo in the chambers of my heart and I hug the pillow tighter. I imagine my arms wrapped around him as his scent fills each alveolus in my lungs.

Within minutes, my eyes grow heavy and drift shut as I dream about beaches and sunsets and giant ever-green trees.

Thirteen years ago

SUMMER WAS ONCE my favorite time of year. Now it officially sucks.

It has been two weeks since Gavin left and all I feel is hollow. A mere shell of the girl I was weeks ago.

Talking with him on the phone every day relieves some of the anguish in my heart. But it never fully dissipates. The strangest part of it all… Before Gavin, I was this loner girl. Someone who never cared for the company of others—with the exception of Shelly. Before Gavin, it had never been challenging to sit beneath a tree by myself and get lost in a book. To hang out in my room alone and listen to music. To walk in the park and listen to the leaves rustle and the birds chirp.

Now, I don't want to even imagine sitting beneath *our*

tree when school starts again. It is bad enough Gavin won't be there, but I also don't have Shelly to hang with since she goes to another school. Listening to music hasn't been the same and I have no desire to step foot outside unless absolutely necessary.

I reach for my sketch pad and pencils and drag them closer. For the next two hours, I get lost in art. At least with art, I create whatever I feel. Art doesn't have to be rainbows or cheeriness or the sunny side of life. It can be anything at any given time. Emotion spilled on paper or canvas and up for interpretation.

When I finish, I dust off the page and take in my drawing. The graphite dons the page in sharp lines and subtle smudges. The scent of pencil shavings pricks my nose. A layer of shiny carbon coats the edges of my palms and several fingertips.

On the page, I drew a beach sunset with a silhouette couple walking hand in hand by the water. In the bottom right corner, I scribble the signature I add to all my art pieces. Before I fold it into thirds, a tear slips from my eye and lands on the page.

I don't wipe it away. I let it stay and bleed through the paper, knowing Gavin will see it when I mail it to him.

On a piece of notebook paper, I start writing a letter to Gavin. Although we talk on the phone regularly, there is something different about sending him drawings or pictures and letters. Like I am sending a physical piece of myself to him. Something for him to hold in his hands when he can't hold me. Something he can look at in the future when he needs me with him. A form of solace in our time apart.

Gavin,

I miss you so much. Sunsets aren't the same without you by my side.

And I'm so tired of everyone asking me if I'm okay. Why would they think I'm okay? My boyfriend, the love of my life, just got shipped off to California. I mean… would they be alright if it happened to them?

I seriously doubt it.

Have you gotten your room situated yet? I know it'll never be like your room here, but maybe you can make it as close as possible.

Thanks for sending me the picture of the California sunset. It's definitely a different view than anywhere here. I hope we can share the sunsets there together sometime. More to add to our memories.

Have I mentioned how Shelly has been following me around all summer like a lost puppy? It's annoying as fuck.

I know she means well, but is it wrong for me to not want to be around anyone else right now?

Whatever. I don't really care what anyone else thinks. All I know is this sucks.

It's like I'm hyperventilating all the time. I'm never able to catch my breath. And it's like my heart is literally missing. If I thumped on my chest, I wouldn't be surprised if it sounded like tapping on a watermelon.

Anyway. The point of these letters isn't to depress you. You miss me as much as I miss you. I just wish I could hug you. You give the best hugs. Did I ever tell you that? No other hug on earth compares to yours. It's warmth and peace and home all wrapped up in the perfect package.

Fuck! I'm crying again. I am sick and tired of crying. My eyes hurt. They're always red and puffy and I have to hide them behind big sunglasses everywhere I go.

This really fucking sucks!

I really hope you're able to come home sometime during the summer. Even if it's just for a long weekend. I'm not picky and will take whatever I get.

Okay, I'll wrap this up. In a few hours, you'll call me and we'll talk until we're forced to hang up. But I never want to hang up. Ever.

I love you so much!

Cora

· · ·

I trifold the letter and stuff it in an envelope, along with the drawing. After I address it, I ask Mom for a stamp and then walk it out to the mailbox. I place it in the mailbox like it's my most prized possession. And for good measure, I press my palm over the envelope and send a piece of myself with the envelope to Gavin.

When I walk back inside, Mom tries to lure me into the kitchen. "Want to make cookies with me?"

Do I look like I'm five and I want to lick the dough from the mixer blades? But I don't say that because I know she is only trying to lift my spirits. She has been trying since Gavin told me they were moving. And more so since the day his parents put him on the plane. I am grateful to have her as my mom, but her love will never be the same as what I give and receive from Gavin.

She means well, and I love her greatly for that, but I just don't see how making cookies will make up for losing someone.

"No thanks, Mom."

I walk back to my bedroom, lay on my bed and curl into a fetal position. I hug my phone to my chest and close my eyes. It won't be long before Gavin calls, but until then I just want to sleep. Sleep away all the minutes and hours and days between when I get to talk with him again. Sleep away every tick of the clock until I get to see him again. And hopefully that day arrives soon.

Present

Is this what dying feels like?

All the years spent apart from Cora and I never felt as horrible as I do now. Did I miss her every goddamn day? Hell yes, I did. Seconds felt like years and years felt like centuries. Did I want to kick myself in the balls for the choices I made? More often than not. Do I regret my idiocy? More than ever.

But the past cannot be changed. It is what it is. No use dwelling on what has come to pass. The future… now that is something I have more control over. Or at least I hope I do.

My stomach churns as I picture her on the ground crying. I stop breathing. Clutch my chest because it feels like I am having a fucking heart attack. Fear rips through me and shreds my insides. And I let the feeling consume me. Let it slither through my veins and take me over. Let the pain settle in my bones. Because seeing Cora in that state was like having someone throw mace-coated sand in your eyes. And I deserve to suffer for not sharing everything with her.

I will accept my punishment. Will let it weigh me down temporarily. Because our relationship can only go up from here.

Since leaving her house yesterday, I have made a new best friend. The porcelain throne in my suite and I have spent quite a bit of time together. I keep telling her I want to see other people, but she is a persistent bitch. As is my stomach, which has kept nothing down.

I press a loose fist to my mouth as I stand beside the bed. I close my eyes and take a deep breath. For the love of all that is holy, please do not let me throw up again. One—I don't like it. I loathe it with a passion. Two—my body cannot handle much more of this. My head hurts from all the dry heaving. Lips are dry as fuck and starting to crack. Throat feels as if a carpenter scraped a layer of tissue off with sandpaper.

I take a few more deep, methodical breaths and am thankful when my stomach finally calms.

I resume packing my suitcase, but the whole act is robotic. Pull from hanger. Fold clothing into a shape other than a ball. Put in suitcase. Repeat. Shoes set inside. Brush. Toothpaste. Toothbrush. Razor. Hygiene products zipped in a bag.

After everything from the closet, dresser, and bathroom are packed up, I walk around the remainder of the room and do a small search. Inspect the kitchen area and small living space. When I get to the couch and table, I lift the cushions like I usually do when I travel. All it takes is one time losing something to develop weird habits like this. And when I hold the seat cushion up, something shiny catches my attention.

I reach for it and discover the shiny object is a hair clip. One that had been in Cora's hair earlier and she took out when we got to my hotel room. She must have slipped it in her pocket and it fell out when we were watching television.

I turn the small clip over in my hand again and again, studying the intricate design. It's nothing girly. Just a simple metal clip with a simple purpose. But it belongs to her.

Cora has never been a girly-girl. But she has never been a complete tomboy either. She resides somewhere in the middle and is absolutely perfect. A girl... A woman not afraid to sweat or get her hands dirty or belch around her friends. A woman who gives as good as she gets and isn't afraid to speak her mind and sees the world as a piece of art. A stunning woman that still puts on a dash of makeup and occasionally wears dresses and fixes her hair with hair clips.

I stare at the clip—a mix of girly and punk rock and hard rock. One-hundred-percent Cora.

I tuck the clip in the pocket of my jeans in the suitcase. When I get home, I will add it to our box. A box that isn't as full as it would have been if we had kept in contact over the years. If *I* had kept in contact with her.

Once my temporary life in Clearwater is packed up, I roll my suitcase to the elevator and press the down button. I step into the car and head for the ground floor. I walk past the front desk and give a courtesy wave on my way to the exit. This is it. After I walk out this door, I am headed back to California.

But not for long.

"Did you already schedule a ride, sir?" the valet asks.

"Yeah. They should be here soon."

"Very well, sir. Have a safe trip home." My body recoils a little at the word *home*.

"Thanks," I tell him, not wanting to be impolite.

When I return to Cora, I will be home. We will be home once I fix my mess and we are together again. Because Cora is home. Always has been. Always will be. Nothing can change that.

The Uber driver picks me up and heads for the Tampa airport. He shoots the shit with me during the entire ride. More than once, I want to tell him I would prefer a quiet drive. But I don't. It's not this guy's fault I am in a foul mood. It's not his fault I left out important details of a favor I did for a friend. And it's not his fault that my so-called friend took said favor and used it as a weapon, attempting to kill the best thing in my life for her own selfish reasons.

Unforgettable. Unforgivable.

When he pulls over at the airport drop-off, I thank the driver after he hands me my suitcase. The doors whoosh open and a wall of cool air hits me as I enter the airport. Weaving through the sea of bodies, I head to the baggage check area. Once I finish checking my luggage, I head upstairs to the gates and TSA checkpoint.

Thirty minutes later, I slip my shoes back on and walk toward the gate. I stop at one of the restaurants and order something small to eat. While I wait, I open the text history between me and Cora. Does this make me a glutton for punishment? Probably, but I don't fucking care.

I have messaged her several times since she got in her car and drove away from me on the beach two nights ago. Most of them say the same thing. *I'm sorry. How are you? I miss you. I love you.*

But she never responds to a single one of them. Not that I really expect her to. If our roles were reversed, I wouldn't do anything different.

Regardless of her lack of response, I type out another text to her. And I will type out many more between now and when I return. Because I will return.

Gavin: Just wanted to let you know I'm at the airport.

When I get back to Cali, I'm fixing all this. All of it. Then I'll be back. I love you. I miss you.

My food arrives and I eat it, not really tasting it. But I repeatedly tell my stomach to keep it down. At least until I land in Los Angeles.

Minutes later, the airport announcement over the intercom says my plane has started boarding. I file into the boarding line and shuffle onto the plane. Once in my seat, I put my earbuds in and shut my eyes. My stomach twists and my palms break out in sweat, but for very different reasons than when I left Los Angeles. This time, the panic forms out of fear.

Fear that I won't be able to fix my mistakes when I land in California. Fear that I won't be able to return to Cora like I desperately want to. And worst of all, fear that she won't take me back when I do return to Florida. Because no matter what happens, I am coming back. Even if it means I have nothing.

The moment I deplane in California, I am a man on a mission. After I text Cora and let her know I landed safely, I bolt from the terminal and head for the baggage claim. As per usual, the airport is a madhouse.

When people bump me along the way, I am more vocal about my irritation than usual. "Fucking asshole" leaves my lips far more often than not. People need to learn some damn etiquette—like moving aside if you plan to text or check apps on your phone. *For the love of God, show some fucking respect.*

And the second I step foot outside the airport, for the first time in years, Los Angeles feels nothing like home. Like the very first time I arrived. If anything, now it feels like a cesspool of hungry and desperate people. A façade disguising itself as reality. And I have no desire to be a part of it.

I was brought here out of obligation, but why did I stay so long? This question has cycled through my head countless times over the last week. Haunted me every waking minute.

Why?

I have been financially secure for years. So why didn't I leave then? Why didn't I pack up everything I own and move back to Florida when I could have? Moving would have been easy. Too easy.

But I hadn't moved for several reasons.

Until a week and a half ago, I hadn't spoken with Cora in years. It wasn't to intentionally hurt her. More like I thought I was doing the right thing when I couldn't see me making it back to her. So, I was doing right by her. At least that is what I told myself. I was letting her go. Letting her move on and find love again.

Only I didn't share that with her. I made the decision all on my own. Because I figured a clean break was the best way. For obvious reasons, I am an idiot. Live and learn, I suppose.

When I get in the Uber, I tell the driver I would like some quiet. I need time to think, to strategize. And I can't do that while a bored driver shoots the shit with me. Thankfully, he respects my request.

After battling late-day traffic, the driver pulls into Mom's driveway on the outskirts of Burbank. I thank the driver, grab my luggage and walk up to the house. Mom's house looks much the same as it did thirteen years ago when we moved to California. The only difference is the paint has faded slightly, the plants have been swapped for more colorful versions, and the tree in the front yard is a little taller and bushier.

Although I have adjusted to Mom living here, this house has still never felt like home. Just a layover until my path realigned.

Maybe I should have messaged Mom before just showing up on her doorstep. She will probably think me crazy. Question me endlessly. Popping up here is nowhere near my norm. Whatever. Perhaps I am going crazy. But if being crazy equals being happy, consider me certifiable.

I punch my code into the door lock and step inside.

The moment I pass the threshold, the scent of curry and bell peppers and grilled chicken attacks my nose. A second later, my stomach growls in response. Obviously, the airport food didn't hold me over long.

"Mom?" I call out.

"Gavin, is that you?"

Every time she asks that, it makes me laugh. Does she have other children I am unaware of? Better yet, is there another guy in her life that could be walking through the door? The latter never crossed my mind until now. I wouldn't expect my mom to remain celibate after Dad passed, but she still wears her wedding jewelry. Wonder if I need to give her the okay to move on? If I need to tell her it is okay to find love again. That I am okay with her loving someone besides Dad.

Maybe another time.

"Yeah, Mom. Are you in the kitchen?" I ask as I walk in that direction. I figure I will ask a stupid question in return. With all the deliciousness floating through the air, she is either cooking or just sitting down to eat.

The second I round the corner and the kitchen comes into view, the grilled peppers and spices hit me full force. My stomach bellows out and constricts, and I pat my abdomen. *Calm down, we will eat soon.*

"Hey, honey. What are you doing here?" She smiles, wraps me in her embrace, and I squeeze her a little harder than usual. "Is everything okay?" Concern laces her voice since I have yet to let her go.

I give her one last squeeze, take a deep breath, then let her go. She steps back to the stove, but has her eyes on me. "No, everything's not okay. I just flew back from Clearwater."

In front of me, Mom freezes with the spoon mid-air above the pan. Her eyes search mine, looking for clues as to what I am thinking, before pinching tightly with sadness. "Oh, Gavin. Was that where your shoot was?"

"Yeah. I didn't think I'd see her. But I was so far off base. Mom… she was the photographer for my shoot."

Mom sets the spoon on the rest and comes to stand beside me. She rubs my back, trying to soothe away my pain. She remembers, all too well, my rebellious days after we moved to California. The torment I endured and inflicted on everyone around me.

"What can I do?"

I turn to her and hug her again. When I release her, I relay my plan to her. And I tell her what happened in Clearwater with Alyson and Layla. How both of them behaved as if their needs and desires supersede mine—even with me in the epicenter.

The fire in Mom's eyes is like nothing I have seen before. Even with all the shit I put her through, she never showed this side. At least not to me. Her cheeks burn bright red as she balls her fingers into tight fists at her side. Right now, Mom is as livid as I am. If not more.

"I'm moving back, Mom. But I have a lot of work ahead of me."

The fire leaves her eyes and is replaced with a gentle smile. "Please tell me what I can do to help. Of course, I'll miss you, but I understand. Your heart never left Florida, honey. Not once."

Since Dad passed away two years ago, Mom and I have grown much closer. For a little while, I let go of the anger and resentment I held toward her. Once I understood she had no choice—take the promotion or possibly lose her job—my forgiveness was easier to dole out.

"True. But I messed up, Mom. I don't know if she'll forgive me."

Mom walks over to the stove and turns off the burner. She grabs two bowls from the cabinet and portions us both some food. We walk over to the small, four-seater dining table and sit. She sets a bowl in front of me before speaking.

When her eyes meet mine, they are serious and determined. "Gavin... Don't stay away and wonder what if this or what if that. If there is one thing losing your father taught me, it's that life is much shorter than we give it credit for. You have to do things now, while you still can. There are so many things your father and I didn't get to do together. Things I will never get to do with him. And I'm fully aware he'd want me to keep living my life. To find someone else who brings me happiness. But I'm not ready for that. It's too soon. Maybe one day..."

I reach across the table and take her hand. "When

you're ready, Mom. It's okay if that doesn't happen for many years to come. Or if it happens sooner than you expect. Anyone who says otherwise is an asshole."

"Gavin," Mom scolds. I shrug her off. "Anyway. You and Cora are young. You have what looks like a lifetime ahead of you. But I thought the same with your father. So, I chose to work hard and save for us to do everything after retirement. But we can't predict the future. I never thought I'd be spending my retirement without your father. It's a hard pill to swallow. And it's not something I want for you. To live in regret. So whatever I can do to help you, let me know. Because your happiness matters more than anything else in my world."

I give her hand a gentle squeeze. "Thanks, Mom. You always say what I need to hear. And after I sort out all the details tomorrow, I'll let you know."

Silence rings around us a moment, but soon Mom and I fall into easy conversation. She talks about work and some new software they are developing to detect specific heart defects in the womb. Some new, experimental noninvasive technology. I listen to every word she says, but a lot of what she tells me is gibberish. A strange blend of medical terminology and techie talk. But it's my mom, so I pay attention to every detail. I smile at her excitement.

When she finishes her story, I tell her about the shoot in Clearwater for Global Beach Magazine. How the magazine will reach major cities across the world. I also let her know I have no doubts about finding a new agent, especially after this shoot. Then I share the last shoot I plan to do here. That it involves Layla. Alyson hasn't told me what the shoot is for yet, but I can only assume it's something to do with couples. If that happens to be the case, I will be speaking with that photographer the moment I arrive on set.

After we finish eating, Mom drives me to my house. We exchange hugs and promises to keep in contact throughout the week. I unlock the front door and wave at Mom as she backs out of the driveway. I stand in the darkness a moment and breathe in the stale air and vacancy around me. When I flip the light on, I scan the empty and soulless house I have lived in for the last eight years.

Then I drop to my knees and cry. "I'm finally going home."

THE SUN BURNS fiery as it collides with the horizon.

Over the last week, I have visited the beach every evening. Sat in the same exact spot and nestled my feet in the warm sand. Watched the sun plummet into the water and fizzle into darkness. Smelled the mustiness of the dampened earth. Felt the salty breeze brush against my skin and whip my hair across my face.

Every night is different. The way the sun glows, how the sky changes colors, the scents in the air and on my skin, the sounds of the waves crashing or people chatting, how the breeze fluctuates. All of it. One night, I sat here in the rain. Actually, it was a downpour. But I refused to leave. If anything, I compared the changes in the atmosphere to the temperance of my mood. Like Mother Earth was going through mood swings and taking me on the journey. And I plan to embrace every leg of said journey.

A half hour after the sun is no longer visible, I rise from the sand and walk back toward my car. The drive home is forgotten, and at times I am surprised I make it home in one piece. I recall getting in my car and parking in the driveway, but nothing in between. Every day is the same.

I unlock the back door and flip on the lights. The scent of daily flower deliveries dying on my kitchen counter permeates the air. For the last five days, a new bouquet of flowers has arrived on my front doorstep. Red roses. White roses. Yellow roses. A mixed variety of roses. And a mixed variety of non-roses.

Each bouquet from my mom and Shelly's florist shop. Each bouquet sent with a small note. And I read each one of them. Absorb all the words. Unlike the text messages I continue to get from Gavin.

The notes sweet and short.

I miss you, baby.

Sunsets are never the same without you.

Tu es les étoiles de ma lune.

Can we watch Lord of the Rings on repeat for a week straight?

Soon, baby. Soon.

Surely, my mom and Shelly are enjoying Gavin's whole charade a little more than most people. And as bad as my house started smelling yesterday, I can't throw any of the flowers away. I just can't. Maybe I should dry them. Drying them would at least eliminate the funk in the air.

Luna weaves figure eights between my legs, purring and mewling as we head toward her bowl. After I give her a scoop of food and a few pets, I head to my room to change clothes. I love the scent of the beach—it conjures up so many wonderful memories—but I don't enjoy the constant sand on my skin. Beach sand is nature's equivalent to glitter.

A few days ago, Shelly stated we were going out. There was no asking and I wasn't allowed to refuse. Everyone was going and we were visiting the nightclub Micah works at in Tampa. Although I didn't want to go, I had no energy to fight Shelly. So I caved. It wasn't worth the argument.

I riffle through my closet and grab a pair of black skinny jeans and an equally black short-sleeve top. On a normal night, I would brush my hair and make myself look presentable. But since I currently give no fucks… I drag my hair up, combing it with my fingers, and securing it with an elastic band. It's sloppy and tired looking and I don't give a shit. If Shelly wants to force me to go out, she will suffer the consequences of my appearance.

Undoubtedly, Shelly will give me a ration of shit, but whatever. She can suck it up like I am.

Minutes later, a knock raps at the door. "It's open," I scream, louder than necessary.

The door opens and three pairs of feet trample across my wood floor. I remain on the couch, staring at the unlit fireplace. Visually tracing the rough grain of the chopped raw wood in the firebox. Pondering if I will ever get to light a fire and snuggle close to Gavin. I briefly close my eyes and take a deep breath. Nowadays, no breaths seem deep enough.

"Why the hell is your back door unlocked?" Shelly asks in her best motherly tone.

And I don't want to listen to her lecture me, just because it is all I have heard for days. If she felt an inkling of what I do, she wouldn't bother with such frivolity. "Because I've only been home for fifteen minutes and knew you guys would be here soon."

Shelly walks over to me and points her finger in my face, her other hand on her hip. "That's no excuse. Lock your freaking door."

I shake my head at her. "Yeah, sure thing *Mom.*"

Erin and Jonas walk over and stand beside Shelly. I

scan them head to toe. Everyone looks great. Hair, attire, overall presence. Me? Looks like I rolled out of bed five seconds ago. But I am not out to impress anyone, so who cares. If people stare, let them.

"You ready to go?" Jonas asks, voice soft with a hint of concern.

"Yeah, let me *lock up* and we can go." I smirk at Shelly and rise from the couch. I give Luna a couple pets and kisses, then we head out.

The drive to Tampa is a blur. Traffic is busy as usual, but I just stare at the lights along the highway. Shelly, Erin, and Jonas try to include me in more than one conversation, but I wiggle my way out of each one. Nothing I have to say matters right now, so it is better just to stay silent and stare out the window.

After we find a place to park, we walk down the sidewalk to the club. Music shakes the walls of the surrounding buildings. Car exhaust floats in the air. Bright headlights blind us as we head to the club's entrance. And I am numb to it all.

Once inside, we find a tall tabletop with stools near the bar. Jonas goes to the bar and buys us all a round. When he returns with our drinks, I practically chug the entire beer. Tonight will be a long night. One of many, unfortunately.

Forty-five minutes and three more beers later, I am somewhere between tipsy and drunk. And for the first time since we arrived, I listen to the music playing. Some electronic dance music I haven't heard before. The beat holds my attention while the bass resonates in my bones. If I wasn't in loner mode, I would head out to the dance floor and give everyone the show of their life. But thankfully, some microscopic piece of logic still resides inside me.

Micah comes over to the table and shoots the shit with Jonas for a few minutes. Moments later, Jonas, Shelly, and Erin get up and go out to the dance floor. Leaving me alone with Micah. Who has hated me since Shelly and I became friends in the third grade. But the way he regards me right now is different. A sort of sympathy residing in the lines of his face. Sympathy he has never directed at me a day in his life.

"How are you?" Micah leans over and asks.

I bring the bottle to my mouth and finish off my beer. "Tired of people asking me how I am. You?"

"I've been better." I catch him glancing over at a woman behind the bar. She's pretty—simple makeup, darker blonde hair piled high on top of her head, a smile that would light up the night sky.

"Who is she?" I openly point at the woman behind the bar.

"Could you please stop pointing?" A few seconds after I comply, he continues. "That's Peyton. She's the new bartender."

"And how long have you been in love with her?"

If Micah had a drink, he would have spit it across the room. Did I hit the nail on the head or what?

"I'm sorry, what? She's only been working here for a couple weeks."

"The length of time she's worked here and how you feel about her are irrelevant. How long have you been in love with her?"

He stares at me like I have two heads. "You're right, it's irrelevant. But you know what isn't? You and Gavin."

I roll my eyes. Nice change of subject. One I cannot ignore or evade. "Ugh, can you please not join the *Save Cora and Gavin* party? If someone isn't talking to me about it every day, the daily flower deliveries are. Isn't it okay for me to just want to go bury myself in blankets and darkness?"

"Seems you are," he states, lifting his chin toward my hair. "Your hair looks like it hasn't seen a brush in weeks. And I know you love rocking the black, but not every day is a funeral."

"You don't get to judge me," I say, pointing my finger in his face. "Black is life. And maybe I feel like death every day. Why do you fucking care?"

He sighs and slumps forward. "Normally, I wouldn't care. But since I talk to Gavin every single goddamn day now, it seems caring is my new middle name." He cocks his head and plasters on a pissy smile.

Gavin and Micah are speaking to each other every day. What the hell are they talking about? Me? Us? There is no us. There hasn't been an "us" in thirteen years. And especially when he decided to stop returning my calls or responding to my letters shortly after he moved away. No matter how much time has passed, those memories still sting. Burn. Char.

"You guys talk that often?" I mumble, staring down at my beer bottle.

"Yeah. He's got a lot happening all at once. Cora…" I glance up at Micah when he says my name. His expression shifts to something more sullen. "He hurt you, I get it. Believe me. But you two need to talk. Really talk. If you don't want to speak to him on the phone, at least respond to one of the million texts he's sent you. Of all people, I figured you'd be the first person to listen. You don't need to explain anything to me, but don't shut him out. Not when he's doing everything within his power to make things right. Not when he's doing everything to come back to you."

Over and over, Gavin told me he would fix this. Told me he would come back to me. But I had heard those words before. Granted, we were kids and didn't have the means to follow through. But like I told Gavin before, actions were what I needed. Lies are made up of words just like truths. And other than flowers, love notes, and his constant reaching out to me, I haven't actually *seen* his actions.

"I'll think about it. But I make no guarantees. I've been dealing with a lot on my end too."

"Like I said, I get it. I've been burned in the past."

And that is the most personal thing Micah has ever shared with me. This whole conversation is surreal. Maybe whoever burned Micah made him realize that being a dick wasn't all it is cracked up to be. Hallelujah!

Shelly, Erin, and Jonas return to the table. They laugh about something, sweat shining on their skin under the multicolored lights. Seconds after their return, Micah slips away. Goes back behind the bar and wistfully side-eyes the new bartender.

I repeat Micah's words in my head. Gavin is fixing things. Gavin is doing everything to come back.

To Florida.

To me.

And the light that snuffed out in my heart a week and a half ago, it flickers for a second. A blip. But sometimes, a blip is all it takes. Sometimes, a blip is what turns darkness into light.

Thirteen years ago

"I'm sorry, Gavin. We just don't have the money to let you fly back to Florida right now," Mom says with a sad smile.

Although she is trying to empathize with me, she has no idea how I feel. And I don't know what upsets me more—the fact I can't fly back to see Cora or that Mom plays the *I understand* card. "But you promised, Mom," I yell across the room, nails biting my palms.

"Don't you take that tone with me. And I never *promised* you'd be able to fly back this summer. I said we would see. And it's not possible right now. I'm sorry."

I storm off to my bedroom, slam the door behind me and lock the handle. "I hate you!" I scream at the walls as I fist my hands in my hair.

"Gavin! Come back out here and apologize to your mother! Now!" Dad stands on the other side of the door, banging.

"Fuck you! Both of you!"

I pick up my desk chair and throw it across the room. One of the legs shatters on impact and I stare at the rubble. A moment later, I punch a hole in the wall beside my bed. Then I collapse on the bed and cry into the comforter.

I lay on my side and draw my legs to my chest. Hours pass and all I can do is lie here and cry. Cry until my eyes burn and my throat numbs. This is utter bullshit. They promised me I would be able to fly back to Florida during the summer. They promised I would be able to see Cora soon after we settled.

But their promises are lies.

It has been a fucking month. We are pretty fucking settled. Although, I don't think I will ever settle here. Everything about this place feels like a death sentence. A prison cell keeping me away from the one person I want more than anything. And why did they make a promise they never had any intention of fulfilling? Just to pacify me? If that's the case, I am more pissed.

Grabbing my phone from my back pocket, I call Cora. Hearing her will settle the anger inside me. Cora has always held the elixir to my soul.

"Hey, Gavin." Her voice perky and happy when she answers. This is exactly what I need right now. Just her.

"Hey, baby. I miss you."

"I miss you, too. Did you talk to your parents? Are you flying back soon?"

The hope in her voice echoes through the line. And I hate that I am about to destroy it. Well, my parents are destroying it. But I am the bearer of the bad news, and I hate it more than anything. Hate that I can't give her—us —better news.

"Yeah, I talked to them."

"And?"

"And they said we don't have the money right now. That there's no way I can fly back this summer."

"Oh," she whispers. And the disappointment is evident in that single word. "Oh. Well, that sucks."

"That's putting it nicely. I told them I fucking hate them."

We stay on the phone—silent—for a moment. She tries to muffle the sound, but I hear her crying. And my heart shatters further because there is not a goddamn thing I can do to make this better. I hate that I can't be there with her. I hate how helpless I feel. That I have no way to console her. To hug her close and kiss her hair. Rub a hand up and down her back, over the back of her head as I press her to my chest. This whole situation is such fucking bullshit.

"Gavin?"

"Yeah, baby?"

"Please don't hate your parents. It's your mom's job

that did this, not her specifically. Your Mom would never intentionally hurt you or us." She chokes out the words and I hate that she is fighting her tears to say nice things about my parents.

But she is right and I know it. Though, I don't know who else to blame for us moving so far away. I am drowning and no one is jumping in to save me. No one tosses me a life preserver.

"I don't really hate them. It's this whole situation that I hate. But I have no other way to express how it's making me feel."

Silence steals the air between us again. But the silence is not uncomfortable. Never has been with Cora. If anything, it calms me. Settles my soul. Gives a peace only she provides.

"Can we talk about something else? Anything else? I don't care what it is," she says. "Have you been to the beach out there yet?"

I love how she knows my favorite place on earth. How she knows it is the one place where I feel solace, other than with her. How she understands my love for the water, the sand, the comfort.

"We went to the beach for the first time a few days ago. It's not the same as the beaches at home."

"How so?"

"The sand grains are bigger. And the water is fucking cold, even in the middle of summer. I didn't get in past my knees. And even that only lasted a few minutes."

"Did you get to stay and watch the sunset?"

God, I love her. Love how she knows me, inside and out. Love how she soothes me so easily. Sunsets are the best, but they will never be the same without her. If I never saw another sunset, but was able to see her again, I would be one-hundred-percent okay with that. Without her, a sunset is just a ball of fire disappearing from sight. Sunsets hold no magic without Cora at my side.

"No, baby. My parents didn't want to stay that late. But maybe we'll get to watch a California sunset together one day."

"We *will* get to watch one together. More than one." The optimism in her voice spreads warmth from the center of my chest to the tips of my fingers and toes.

"One day. Until that day comes though, you watch the sunsets there for me. And I'll watch them here. But I'd rather wait until you're with me."

"Me too."

For the next hour, we talk about random things. Places we went together. Things that made us laugh. And it's not until I hear her yawn that I realize it is past midnight in Florida. Another shitty side effect of this move—the three-hour time zone difference. I would stay up all night and talk with her. But we are both tired, more mentally and emotionally than physically.

"I should let you go to bed, baby."

"As sweet as that is, it doesn't matter much. I only

sleep a couple hours a night now. But I guess you're right."

I don't want to hang up the phone. Even if we sit here and say nothing for hours on end, just hearing her breathe on the other end makes me feel at home.

As if she can read my mind, even with several states and thousands of miles between us, she says, "Maybe we can just lay down and set our phones on our pillows. We can pretend that we're side by side."

"That sounds like the best idea I've heard in days," I tell her as I fight the tears stinging the backs of my eyes.

And for the next two hours, I listen to her sleep. Listen to her soft breaths and occasional sleep-spoken words. Words like *love* and *soon* and *forever*.

Present

THIS SHOOT with Layla is exactly what I thought it would be. A shit show to flaunt our "relationship." Well I hope she is prepared for said relationship—as well as our friendship—to end. Because the line has been drawn and this is definitely over. Hope she enjoyed riding in my wake while it lasted.

The photographer directs us here and there and I follow through as if nothing has changed. But everything has changed. And in about fifteen minutes, Layla and Alyson are about to find out exactly how much it has changed. In less than a minute, everything in their world will tip on its axis. As it did mine.

They shouldn't have pushed me here. They should have let me pursue my relationship with Cora. Live my life how I want. But neither of them seemed capable of handling life when I wasn't improving theirs. Now... now there is no other option. They did this and now they will pay the consequences.

A few more clicks of the camera and the photographer announces the shoot is a wrap. As soon as those words are spoken, I distance myself from Layla. And she notices immediately.

"You okay?" Layla asks as she approaches me.

I slip a hoodie over my head before chugging my water dry. During the whole process, Layla stands a foot away and regards my lack of speech and eye contact. Good. I hope it makes her sweat. Hope it makes her question why I have been so standoffish. Hope it unsettles and worries her. It should.

But she won't have to question much of anything in a moment. Shit... meet fan.

Out of the corner of my eye, I spy Alyson walking toward us. I drag in a deep breath and prepare for what will happen next. If I know these two women well enough, one will go into hysterics while the other throws a rage fit. Not that I care, but let's see how right I am.

"Gavin. Layla. Great job out there today," Alyson chirps. Her whole demeanor is as it was before we ever went to Florida. Chipper and smiley and completely artificial. Since she has been my agent, I always sensed her artifice. But I passed it off as being out in Los Angeles, and that is how most of the population is.

Now, I see things differently. Now, I see she only cares about me for one reason. My signature on her paycheck.

Alyson starts scrolling through her phone and ignoring Layla and me. As she has done a thousand times prior. So, I steel myself and start the inevitable.

"Alyson. Layla. We need to talk."

Layla stares at me, her amber resin eyes asking me question after question. But I ignore her and stare at Alyson, who has yet to look up from her phone. With each passing second, the fact that she continues to ignore me pisses me off further. So to grab her attention, I opt to snap my fingers in her face.

When she finally looks up from her still lit-up phone screen, irritation rests on her face. Irritation for me disrupting her. But I don't give a fuck.

Welcome to the club of pissed-off people, my name is Gavin.

"Gavin, I was just reading an email for another shoot. If you would've waited another—" Alyson attempts to hold the floor, but I cut her off.

"Stop," I shout. My voice bounces around the small studio. The eyes of crew members still in the room look our way. But I don't give a shit. I am over this. More than over it. "As I said a moment ago, we need to talk. The three of us."

"I heard you, Gavin. Can it not wait? I have other appointments I need to get to." As she says the words, she flicks her wrist and glances down at the gold and diamond watch on her arm. This irritates me more.

"No, Alyson. It cannot wait," I seethe.

She locks her phone and rests her hands on her hips. She purses her lips and regards me as if I am behaving like a stubborn child. Obviously, she has forgotten her place in this world. Has forgotten the fact that she only has a paycheck because I grant her such a privilege. Sure, she has other clients, but none of them are as big as I am or as fruitful to her bank account. If anything, she should be vying for my attention. Doing whatever makes me happy.

"Well, spit it out. As I said, I have other appointments to get to."

Beside me, Layla starts biting her fingernails. It is such a disgusting habit. One I tried to help her curb time after time. By the time I finish, she probably won't have any nails left.

My eyes dart between the two of them—one worried, the other annoyed. "You're fired," I state firmly, not an ounce of regret in my voice.

Alyson blinks a few times before taking a step back. Confusion mars her face for a beat as she lifts a hand to her chest. "Sorry, I think I may have misheard you. What did you just say?"

I want to laugh and shake my head, but bite my lip and resist the urge. She heard me loud and clear. Just doesn't want to believe it. "You heard me just fine. But if it needs repeating… You. Are. Fired." She jerks her head away as if I slapped her. But before she says another word, I face Layla next. "And you… I don't ever want to see you again. We're done. No more fake engagement. No more friendship. I hope you enjoyed the ride because it's time to exit."

Layla goes wide-eyed and stands speechless. She stares at me slack-jawed as her eyes glaze over. A million thoughts and questions flit across her face, but she remains stoic. After a moment, she finally locates her voice. "This is because of *her*, isn't it?"

I don't owe either of them an explanation after the shit they have put me through, but I answer her anyway. "If I'm being honest, it's not just because of Cora. But yes, Layla, she is the shift that has made this happen. It was a long time coming, and she gave me the push I'd been missing for years."

"You can't do this!" Alyson yells, not caring who heard her outburst. She points her French-manicured nail in my face. "We have a contract." Her eyes light up, hoping she caught me in some loophole I forgot about.

But I didn't forget about our contract. She must have me pegged as an idiot. Joke is on her.

"Actually, I can do this. We *did* have a contract. A contract I had my attorney look over when I told him I wanted to seek a new agent. After some light reading—" I smirk "—it was determined that our contract period ended almost two years ago. But seeing as we had been doing so well together, neither of us paid much attention to that fact. Too bad for you."

Alyson is a deer in the headlights. She has no comeback for the truth I just laid on the table. No rebuttal for the fact that we carried on for an additional two years without signing a new contract. This hiccup is a win for me, and a major loss for her. If she would have continued looking out for my best interests, our business relationship may have continued. But greed took hold. And greed loses in the long run.

While Alyson marinates in the loss of being my agent, I turn and speak to Layla. "You know, we had a great friendship. One I never questioned. We were always there for each other. Had each other's back. But your ego surpassed your morality not too long ago. And the stunt you pulled in Florida… it's unforgivable."

A lone tear rolls down her cheek, her perfect stage makeup not smearing or running. Sadness hits when I question if I should believe this tear or not. As a model, Layla is an actor. She knows how to put on a show for the camera and crowd. Knows how to make people believe what she is selling. So how can I believe this lone tear is real? That it comes from somewhere genuine.

The answer is simple—I can't.

"Gavin," she chokes out and sniffles. "I'm sorry. It's just… Alyson called me and told me what was going on. That you planned to move back to Florida. And I just reacted. I freaked."

I shake my head. "You *just reacted*? You *freaked*?" I laugh at her, incredulous. "No. What you did was behave like a child who didn't get her way. Because if I moved away from you, you wouldn't get to ride my coattails anymore. But instead of talking with me, you chose a different tactic. Chose to be bitter and selfish and vindictive. Too bad it didn't work in your favor."

Her tears flow a little more steadily now. Maybe they are real, but no chance in hell am I letting my guard down enough to question their validity. If my guard goes down, she will push her guilt on me to appease herself.

"Gavin, please," Layla begs. "If our years of friendship mean anything to you—"

"No," I shout. "You don't get to pull the friendship card to manipulate me. After the stunt you pulled, knowing full well what it would do, there is no friendship card anymore. It expired the moment you used me as a pawn in some game to keep me. You know what she means to me, and you used that knowledge as a weapon. Friends don't do shit like that, Layla. Friends congratulate each other when good things happen."

In my periphery, Alyson unlocks her phone and begins to frantically go from screen to screen. I told my attorney I planned to speak with Alyson and Layla after the shoot ended, and gave him an estimated time as to when that would be. By now, he has emailed the termination paperwork to Alyson. A few seconds later, my thoughts are validated when Alyson slaps her hand to her mouth and gasps. As if she did not believe me.

My work here is done. And I have other obligations to attend to. So, without another word, I turn my back on them and walk away. Both women try to garner my attention as I head for the exit, but I ignore them as I push through the door. Already, a major weight lifts from my chest and I breathe a little easier.

Studio lights blind me as a man attaches a small microphone to my shirt. "Mr. Hunt, could you please say a few words so we can test the mic?"

I have the sudden urge to behave like a child with a toy microphone. I tap the mic clipped to my shirt a few times. "Testing. Testing. One, two, three. Can you hear me?"

A woman behind a soundboard with headphones over her ears gives a thumbs up. The man beside me returns the gesture then fidgets with the mic a little more, trying to disguise it behind my shirt. A moment later, he walks off and leaves me to sit on the studio stage alone.

Before I have too much time to ponder how long I

will sit here alone, Janet Maverick sits in the plush armchair beside me. Janet Maverick—one of Hollywood's top reporters. When she talks to a crowd, people listen. And that is the exact reason I came to her. So my story will be heard by the masses.

"Hey, Gavin. How are you today?" Janet asks, genuinely interested.

"Oh, you know. Things aren't so hot. But I'm hoping this interview will be the fresh start to things getting better."

She nods. "I'm sure everything will work out. Just stay positive."

A moment later, the stage crew crowd around us. We are asked to get in position on set. Janet and I are asked to say a few last things for a final check of our mics. Then a woman behind one of several cameras begins counting down with her fingers before pointing at Janet.

"Good evening, Los Angeles. If this is your first time tuning in, I'm Janet Maverick. And you're watching The Heart of Hollywood. Tonight, I am honored to have Gavin Hunt on stage with me." Janet faces me and gives a warm smile. "Welcome, Gavin."

I have been in front of a camera hundreds of times, but in this moment an overwhelming sense of stage fright consumes me. "Thank you, Janet. It's great to be here," I stumble then cough. A stagehand points to a bottle of water beside me, signaling me to drink. Glad someone is looking out for me.

Janet carries on as if there is no reason to panic. As if millions of people aren't flipping on their televisions to watch this very moment. Right now, I envy her this.

"For those of you who aren't familiar with the man beside me… First of all, shame on you," she jokes. "Seriously. Mister Gavin Hunt is a model. You may have seen his work in a magazine or twenty. He has also appeared on the cover of several romance novels. Ladies, check those book covers."

Someone behind the soundboard presses a button and some previously recorded laughter echoes around us.

"But let's get down to the nitty-gritty," Janet says. "Gavin, you just returned from a photo shoot in Florida. How did it go?"

I hold Janet's gaze, doing my best to ignore the cameras and crew focused on us. After a quick inhale, I answer. "The photo shoot was phenomenal. It was nice to return to Florida after being away for so many years."

Janet perks up at this. "Return to Florida? Is that where you're originally from, Gavin?"

"It is. I moved out to California when I was sixteen after my mom received a promotion. This past trip was the first time I'd been back."

She nods, her face studious over my response. "So, what can we look forward to seeing after this shoot?"

"I was doing a shoot for Beach Global Magazine. There will be several images with a new line I'm helping them promote. Casual wear for the beach and city. As well as swimwear and undergarments," I say, waggling my brows.

Janet lays her hand over her heart before fanning herself. "Gavin, you can't just say things like that. Now I'm blushing on national television." She swats me with a small pad of paper.

"The magazine is set to release at the beginning of summer. Make sure you get your copy. I guarantee you won't be disappointed." I wink at her.

"Ladies, you heard it here. Keep your eye on the magazine stands." Janet takes a sip of water, then switches tactics. "Other than work, Gavin, how is life treating you?"

This is why I came here. To expose my life to the masses. Tell my story—the truth as well as the web of lies. I need the façade of what Layla and I had to be uncovered. For all the stories of our perfect "engagement" to be brought out in the light and diminished.

"Well, Janet, things are a bit rough right now," I say.

"Aw, I'm sorry to hear this. What's going on?"

"My trip to Florida ended up becoming more than just a work trip. For the first time in thirteen years, I ran into the love of my life."

Janet gasps and slaps a hand over her mouth, eyes awestruck. "Oh my, Gavin. I don't know what to say. Why has it been so long since you've seen this woman? And wait… what about your engagement?"

The perfect segue into clearing the air. Thank you very much. "That's part of the reason I'm here tonight, Janet. I want to clear the air about a few things. The first thing being my engagement to Layla Hendricks. After running into my high school sweetheart, many things were put into perspective. One of those things being said engagement. An engagement that was done purely for business reasons."

"Well, you are just full of surprises tonight," Janet states.

I nod. "Indeed. Layla and I have been friends since I moved to California. But that's all. My heart has always been in Florida. As my career took off, Layla struggled. Our agent got her shoots with several well-known photographers, but nothing boosted her career. After a year, our agent suggested we pretend to get engaged. That my soaring career would lift hers. So, I agreed. Layla was my friend, and I wanted to help her. But while I was in Florida, that favor and my friendship was taken advantage of. As of today, I have cut all business ties with my agent and Layla. And have also severed my friendship with Ms. Hendricks."

Janet and I sit in silence for several long seconds. Now that I have said my part—gotten the falsehoods of my engagement to Layla off my chest and told the world I am in love with someone else—relief rushes through my veins. A weight that has anchored me in place for years instantly lightens. With such a simple action, I feel a hundred pounds lighter. Now, I need to repair things between me and Cora. And with my level of determination, I will fix us.

"Wow, Gavin. I'm not even sure where to begin. If you don't mind sharing with us, what happened in Florida that sparked this dramatic change? Other than seeing this mystery woman."

I hadn't been given permission to mention Cora's name, so keeping her anonymity is vital. Although, Hollywood will figure out who she is eventually. But until that day arrives, my lips remain sealed.

"Janet, there aren't adequate words to explain what seeing this woman did to me. It's as if my heart started beating again." At my words, Janet and a few of the female crewmembers swoon. The visual adds a smile to my face. "When I was younger, I didn't have a say in my family moving to California. But now, I make all my decisions. And that's why I have chosen to move back to Florida."

Saying the words aloud, announcing them to millions of viewers, sets my pulse to a wild gallop beneath my sternum. But after seeing Cora, after being in the same space as her for a week, there is no possible chance of me staying away. Not anymore. Cora is everything I always wanted. A breath of fresh air. The only person to soothe and satiate my soul. Moving back to Florida is something I should have done years ago. For too long, the flashing lights and starry eyes distracted me. But I have no doubts this is the right choice. Cora has always been the right choice.

"Well, Gavin. I'm not sure I know what else to say. California will miss you. I will miss you," she says, smiling wide.

"You haven't seen the last of me, Janet. I'm not leaving the industry. Just making some personal changes. But you'll still get to glance at my pretty face," I tease.

"Whew. That's good news. I'm not sure how my life would continue if I didn't see you around the city." She pauses, reaching across the space between us and resting her hand on mine. "Thank you for sitting with me today. It was wonderful to see you. Keep us posted on how things go with this mystery woman."

"Will do, Janet. Thank you for having me."

As Janet says her parting words into the camera, I review all the things I need to do in my mental checklist.

Fire Alyson. Check.

Give Layla the boot. Check.

Review my new agent's contract. Still need to do.

Call Micah. Still need to do.

Deal with the house. Work in progress.

As I walk off the stage, my phone dings in my pocket. When I retrieve it, there is a message from the realtor I contacted yesterday. Her timing couldn't be more perfect. And I take it as a sign everything will work out as planned. At least that is what I hope.

"Of course, you can stay with me, man. I'd never leave you on the streets. When do you think you'll get here?" Micah asks.

Not sure why I was worried, but I am so relieved he said yes to me staying at his place until I buy a new house. Micah and I have known each other almost twenty years, but I had my doubts about him agreeing to let me stay. He may be my best and longtime friend, but how he acted around Cora while I was in Florida had me antsy to hear his response. The fact he said yes alleviates another concern.

"Maybe in the next few days or so. The house is under contract and I'll know more tomorrow or the next day. Is it cool if I ship some boxes and my car to your place?"

"Sure thing. Whatever you need. Mi casa es su casa. Just let me know when they'll be here, so I'm home when they arrive."

The sale of my California house is moving much quicker than anticipated. And I took it as yet another sign. The cosmos are rooting for me—for me and Cora. The stars aligning invigorates me, has me doing things at maximum speed. If the forward momentum continues at this pace, I will be back in Florida within a week. Hopefully sooner. Fixing things with Cora can't happen fast enough. Being with her again, especially.

"Thanks, bro. I'll shoot you a text with the shipping info. For now, I'm only sending clothes and necessities. When I find a place, I'll have everything else shipped."

Micah and I talk for a few more minutes, catching up on other things. After we hang up, I go into beast mode. By the end of the day, ninety percent of my house is packed into boxes. Lucky for me, I have never been a packrat. By no means am I a minimalist, but over the years I had no desire to fill my house with endless knick-knacks. I suppose I always knew I would pack things up.

I call the shipping company and set up a time to have the boxes and my car picked up. After, I set up for the remaining boxes and furniture to be shipped to my mom's house. When I told her how quick things were progressing with the sale of my house, she offered her unused two-car garage as storage space.

Everything came together with ease. How can I not believe in fate? Everything continues to line up for us to be together again. If it isn't divinity, I don't know what it is.

But as I lay awake in bed, I question how I will fix things with Cora. As smooth as things are going, a twinge of doubt lingers in the back of my mind. It taunts me and has uncertainty creeping in my veins.

What if she rejects me? Although the chemistry

between us is more than obvious, I hurt her. More than once. Hurt like that doesn't just vanish. What if she doesn't forgive me? The possibility lingers in my thoughts and gnaws at my heart. Because as much as I have done to prove my promise to Cora, the possibility of her not letting me back in still stands. Which begs the question…

What if all this is for nothing?

News travels fast in the photography and modeling circuit.

Only two days have passed since I sent over the finalized photos from Gavin's shoot to the magazine. Riffling through thousands of images of Gavin wasn't easy by any stretch of the imagination, but eventually I selected my top three from each look the magazine wanted. Most of the images I sent aren't my personal favorites—those I kept all for myself—but they are notable and salesworthy photographs.

As I sip on a cup of hot caffeine, I read the fifth email from a local company seeking my photography skills. And I am in complete awe. Doing this photo shoot with Gavin has already opened multiple doors for me. Some doors I wish would have remained closed. The doors trapping my heart and memories in the dark corners of my mind.

I keep thinking of Gavin's promise to return to me. His promise to fix past mistakes and explain all the things I didn't understand. But as each day passes, I wonder if he will follow through with his promises. If the perfume from days' worth of flower deliveries was any indication, he plans to return. The only thought constantly rolling around in my head is how we move forward.

So much of our lives has changed. Adulthood changes people. But so much of what we once had remains untouched.

At one point in our lives, Gavin and I shared everything with each other. There were no secrets between us —intentional or by accidental omission. With the latest revelation—his supposed fake engagement to *her*—I wasn't sure I could give Gavin my trust. I want to believe it is possible for us to get back to where we were years ago. The place where I knew every facet of his life and vice versa.

Because the end of us couldn't be *this*—an ugly, painful, heart-wrenching reality.

The way things are now, they are so different from when we were younger. What I thought was pain at age sixteen is nothing compared to this vacant space beneath my breast bone. At least, back then, I experienced sensation where my heart resided in my chest. Now, my heart feels numb and hollow. The organ still beats, still pumps blood through my veins, but it only does so to keep me in existence. There is no life behind the rhythm. No real purpose. Just a machine doing its job.

My phone pings with an incoming text. Reluctantly, I glance at the screen. Although I haven't responded, Gavin continues to text me updates. Last I heard, he fired his agent and broke off his friendship and fake engagement with *her*. That text brought an actual smile to my face. But we still have a long way to go.

Shelly: You, me, Jonas. Bar. Tonight.

Shelly has always known how to make me smile and laugh. Her simple text does exactly that. Her message short, sweet, and to the point.

As much as I want to be a hermit and hide in my shell of a house, Shelly has the right remedy. A night out with my friends is exactly what I need to boost my mood. To sit amongst the crowd, sip on a beer and listen to people belt out karaoke. The solution to every bad day in history is awkward karaoke.

Cora: Sounds good. What time?
Shelly: Six. We need to grab a good table before the crowd arrives.
Cora: See you at six.

I read through the emails again and decide to accept two of the offers. Respectfully declining the others, I tell them to reach out in the future and check my availability. The two I accept are in the Bay Area. One is for the city of St. Petersburg, who has requested for me to do a cityscape with some patrons. The city is looking to update images for tourism since the city has changed so much in the last five years. They want to show off city life and all the wonderful things the area has to offer. The other offer is for boudoir photos of a couple in Tampa. Details are vague, but enough for me to be comfortable and accept.

After I respond to the emails, I make the mistake of opening the file on my laptop titled "DO NOT OPEN." Because, for some reason, I am a glutton for punishment.

For the next hour, I scroll through photo after photo of Gavin. From the photo shoot, and times when he wasn't paying attention. Frame after frame after frame. Years ago, I had photos of us from high school digitized. Those same images were now parked in this folder. And I cannot force myself to look away.

Click. Click. Click.

Cue the tears. And the burn in my nose. Followed by the clog in my throat.

As each image from our younger years passes over the screen, I cry uglier and harder. I tremble from head to toe as my vision blurs and a tight pinch pierces between my lungs. The onslaught of memories set off the full emotional spectrum and it is pure misery. And I welcome every ounce of it.

At least anguish is better than numbness. At least it reminds me I am still alive. Because some days, I wonder if this is one huge nightmare. Some sick, twisted version of hell. Some days, life is hell.

I wake up on the couch, the blanket cocooning me and Luna purring on my chest. The light of day dims, but the sun is still up. I give Luna a few pets before cuddling her in my arms. After a moment, I bolt upright and Luna hisses at me before scampering off.

"Sorry, Luna."

Shit. What time is it? I told Shelly I would meet her and Jonas at the bar.

I glance at the clock on the kitchen wall, noting it's five-twenty. Flying off the couch, I head for my room and riffle through my closet. Thank goodness the bar is a short drive from the house, otherwise I would be screwed. After picking out a top and a pair of jeans, I jump in the shower and wash away the pool of sorrow I have been swimming in all day.

Once out and dressed, I feed Luna and grab my keys

and wallet. I dash out the door and drive to the bar. Seven minutes later, I park in the lot and step through the bar doors.

I spot Shelly and Jonas at our usual table and walk over to them.

"Hey, you look like shit," Shelly says, not sugar-coating my wayward appearance.

"You really know how to flatter a girl. *Thanks.* I haven't been sleeping much. You're lucky I got a nap in before tonight, otherwise I'd look so much better."

I flip her the middle finger. But she knows I'm teasing her.

"Sorry. You know I call it as I see it," she apologizes with a shrug.

"True. Can we please talk about something else?" I didn't come out to talk about how depressing my life is. Tonight is about having fun and feeling better. If that isn't going to happen, I will just go home and wallow alone.

"Yeah, sorry," Shelly says.

The waitress approaches the table and sets down three beers. Mine is at my lips within a second, half of it down my throat. At this rate, I will be drunk in no time. We order another round and some appetizers.

By the time karaoke starts an hour later, I am some-where between tipsy and drunk. And it is a nice place to be. In this state, not much of anything matters. Life has no issues. No drama. No life-altering decisions need to be made. It's all rainbows and unicorns and horrible singers on small stages.

As some overly primped woman sings the words to Bon Jovi's "You Give Love a Bad Name", I lean on Jonas. His arm wraps around my shoulder and keeps me from teetering off my stool.

Jonas really is a great guy. I hope he happens upon the right woman one day. As much as we went back and forth, part of me always knew nothing more would evolve between us. Jonas has a big heart and will be perfect for a very lucky lady one day. But that lady won't be me. And I hope he knows Shelly and I will need to approve whoever this future mystery woman will be. She will have a lot to live up to.

Jonas presses a kiss to the top of my head. "Are you okay?" he whisper-asks just loud enough for me to hear.

For a second, I nod. But the nod slowly transitions, and soon I shake my head before turning my face into his shoulder.

God, I am sick and tired of crying. My bloodshot eyes ache and feel as if they are swollen to twice their size. My throat scratches every time I speak and throbs with each breath I take. And honestly, I don't know how much more of this I can handle.

Jonas delicately rubs a hand up and down my back. Says soothing words only I hear. Shushes me and tells me everything will be alright. And his kindness has me on the cusp of crying harder, but I resist. There is only so much my body can handle.

Two lackluster karaoke songs later, we all agree to call it a night. We pay our tab before I stumble out the door. Jonas drives me home in my car and Shelly follows us so she can take Jonas back to his Jeep. The drive is short and filled with low-volume rock music from the radio. Jonas doesn't speak up while I lean against the window with my eyes closed. Minutes later, we park in my driveway and shuffle out. Shelly and Jonas walk me inside, hug me goodnight and disappear out the door.

Once alone, I kick off my shoes and peel off my jeans, crawl into bed and curl into a ball. Luna jumps up on the bed and nudges her head against mine. For a beat, I pet her soft fur and a sense of comfort washes over me as she purrs loudly and professes her unconditional love.

"At least you'll stay by my side, pretty girl," I whisper.

As if she understands me, Luna meows in response. I snuggle her into my chest and fall asleep, waking on and off through the night. Throughout the night, dreams of photos and drawings, hand holding and kisses, good-byes and love letters haunt me every hour. As they do every night. And probably will for the rest of my life.

Twelve and a half years ago

TODAY IS the most important day of my life. But it doesn't matter. Not anymore.

On this day two years ago, Gavin and I officially started dating. Before he moved to California, we celebrated every possible relationship milestone. One month. Three months. Six months. One year. But today, on our two-year anniversary, I haven't heard a word from him.

His lack of reaching out to me can easily be blamed on time zone differences. The hour is still early in California, and he is probably sleeping. But a sinking suspicion in my gut tells me it has nothing to do with the time zones. This nerve-laden ache has been getting bigger each day we are apart.

Six months has passed since Gavin left Florida. Six

very long, dark months. The last four… I haven't heard from Gavin at all. No return phone calls or texts. No response to the numerous letters I have mailed him. As if he vanished from the earth. Poof. At one point, I called and asked Mrs. Hunt if Gavin was still alive. She apologized profusely and told me Gavin was not doing well with the transition.

Neither was I, for that matter.

Since Gavin left, life has been complete and utter shit. My mom is lucky if I get out of bed each day. After weeks of tears and depression, Mom and Dad took me to see a therapist. We talked, she prescribed me anti-depressants and that was all she wrote. But pills will never replace my heart. Pills will never make this ache vanish. Only Gavin can do that. And he is gone.

Poof.

As with Gavin, everything I ever loved disappeared. My love for art has been almost nonexistent. School is going down the drain at a rapid pace. The only thing that kept me attending each day was the opportunity to sit under our tree. To trace my fingertips over the carved wood where our initials reside, along with his words only for me. Under that tree was our spot. Will always be our spot. The only physical piece of him I have a connection to every day.

I call Gavin's house and the phone rings twice before Mr. Hunt answers. "Hello?"

I waited as late as possible, so it isn't too early on the

west coast. Currently eight in the morning in California. "Hi, Mr. Hunt. It's Cora. Sorry to call so early. Is Gavin awake?" I pick at the hem of my jeans as I wait, nervous.

"Good morning, sweetheart. It's not too early. But I'm sorry, Gavin isn't home. He stayed over at a friend's house last night."

"Oh," I say, disappointment evident in my tone. "Okay, thank you. I'll try calling his cell phone."

Before I hang up, Mr. Hunt speaks. "Cora? I'm so sorry about everything. I know neither of you is handling this well."

I bite my tongue to avoid crying in the phone. I wonder if he knows how distant Gavin and I have become. Miles and states aren't the only things that separate us now, it is also our lack of connection. Our lack of communication.

Is this what happens when soul mates are ripped apart? They drift and fade and become shells of themselves.

"Thank you, Mr. Hunt," I manage. "Please let Gavin know I called."

"I will, sweetheart. If we don't talk again before, have a happy Thanksgiving," he says.

And I almost lose it on the phone. "You all too." Then I hang up.

I wait a few minutes, gathering my thoughts and emotions. The last thing I want is to call Gavin and cry during our conversation. Although, nowadays I cry more often than not.

Opening Gavin's contact on my phone, I tap the little phone image before bringing the phone to my ear. *First ring.* God, I have missed hearing his voice. *Second ring.* But not more than I have missed his touch. *Third ring.* Or the feel of his lips pressed against mine. *Fourth ring.* And the way he held me close any chance he got. *Voicemail.*

"This is Gavin. Leave me a message. Or don't. I really don't give a shit either way."

Why isn't he answering? By now, it seems as if he purposely avoids me. And I don't know why. Because he won't fucking talk to me.

Beep.

"Hey, Gavin. It's me. Your girlfriend. Although that seems questionable since you haven't spoken to me in four months. Not once. I really miss you. And of all days to not respond to me… guess I should've known you'd find someone else to love. Thanks for having the balls to tell me. Whatever. You probably won't even listen to this. But if you do… Happy anniversary. Hope you have a *great* day."

I hang up and throw my phone across the room, screaming at the top of my lungs. And it's no surprise, no one comes to my room and asks what is wrong. Because Mom and Dad both know. They know what day today is. They know that I have only gotten worse with each passing day. Mom also knows I haven't spoken to Gavin in months. The longer I don't hear from Gavin—let alone see him—the more bitter I become. The more withdrawn I become. Whatever his reason for cutting me off, it would have been nice if he made me privy. As it is, I feel like I have been played.

After screaming a few more times, I rummage through my closet. When I locate my art supplies, I yank them down and cast them across my bedroom floor. For the next few hours, I submerge myself in charcoals and my art pad. My fingertips are coated in black coal, and I am certain my face has streaks from where I scratched my face a couple times.

But it doesn't matter. Nothing fucking matters.

I draw and shade and accentuate. When I finish the first image, I tear it from the pad and start a new piece. This process happens on repeat for hours. By the time I stop, the sun has begun setting. Three finished drawings lay in front of me, another still attached to the pad and left unfinished. I stare at the three images as a tear drips from my chin and splatters on the charcoal.

The first is a replica of the first day I met Gavin. Both of us sitting under our tree, before it was blemished by his pocket knife. Before it was *our* tree. I recall that day and how eager he was to make conversation with me. Continually ignoring him, I read my book and secretly memorized the lines of his face out of the corner of my eye. I listened to his breathing pattern and tried to match mine to it. I glanced down at his hands and watched them fumble as he sat nervously beside me.

The second image is a flashback to two years ago. Of

Gavin and me at the beach, in the water, kissing for the first time. That day was pure magic. No other day compares to how I felt when his lips grazed mine for the first time. Like an incinerator ignited low in my belly, heat spreading throughout my body in the cool Gulf. And no matter who was looking, we stayed like that for hours in the water. Tangled limbs and hungry kisses. On that day, he became mine, and I became his. Forever.

And the third image makes me blush. In this piece, we are topless. Lips locked. Bodies crushed together. Hands in the other's hair and groping body parts. This was us. Exposed and vulnerable and losing ourselves in one another. And the night we lost our virginity. A night that will be forever engraved in my memory. Not just the physicality, but also the way his eyes softened and his breath caught and my name rolled off his tongue.

The more I stare at the drawings, the harder the tears fall. Before too many hit the pages, I swipe them away and fold up the pages. The unfinished page stays attached to the pad—a picture of me now. More like a silhouette. Because all I feel is darkness. Nothingness.

Grabbing one of my school notebooks, I open it to a blank page and write a letter to Gavin. One I hope he reads.

Gavin,

Today is our two-year anniversary. And all I want to do is talk to you. But we haven't talked in so long. Now, I am just empty inside. Lifeless. Moving to California wasn't your fault. You hate it. I hate it. And there is nothing we can do about it.

I called your house earlier and your Dad told me you stayed over at a friend's house. I'm happy you've made new friends out there. And I'm happy you seem to be moving on without me.

I won't bore you with my life. Because it's one big shit show on my end. Maybe I'll start my meds again, so at least I experience some form of happiness. Even if it is fake. Fake is better than nothing at all. Right?

Inside this envelope are three drawings of happier times. After this, I may just burn all my art supplies. Because anything worth capturing doesn't exist anymore. Not since you left. Not since you stopped talking with me.

Why? Why have you stopped talking with and writing me? Did you find someone else already? Was I that easy to forget? Am I not even worth friendship?

I hate myself. I hate my life. Hate that I have given you my heart and you've stomped on it until it turned to dust.

Does your heart feel like a black hole? Because mine does. It feels like this dark, hollow place that sucks all the happiness from the world and demolishes it.

It doesn't matter anymore. None of it does. You. Me. Us. Who were we to think we would see each other again? We're fools. Or at least I'm a fool. Because I believed we would. Believed this separation was a temporary blip in our relationship. Something easily fixed after a little patience.

But it seems I was wrong.

Because it feels like you have moved on without me. Left me to rot with the garbage.

And I'm done. Done spending every second of every day wondering what you're doing. If you care or think about me still. It's pretty obvious what the answer is, especially if you never speak to me. This situation sucks, but I never imagined you'd do this to me. Ghost me.

So, goodbye Gavin. It was my privilege to love you. And maybe one day in the future, I will get the chance again. God, I hope so. Because I will never love anyone the way I love you. If I'm honest, I don't ever want to love anyone else. I'd rather die alone, miserable and frail.

I hope you read this and it makes your heart hurt the same as mine. I hope it makes you shed as many tears as I have. And I hope you find it in your heart to come back to me one day.

Because I will always love you. Forever.

Tu es les étoiles de ma lune.

Cora

I fold the paper into thirds and set it with the drawings as I search the house for a large envelope. When I locate one, I shove the drawings and letter inside, addressing it to Gavin and slapping on too many stamps. A minute later, I walk to the mailbox and place the envelope inside, raising the red flag.

As I walk away from the envelope, I settle into my new reality. A reality where Gavin and Cora don't exist. A reality where love dies and hearts shatter into millions of little fragments. And a reality where nothing matters, because what is the point. What. Is. The. Point?

Present

I STARE off in the distance as my Range Rover is loaded into a freight box with a few boxes of my clothes inside the car. The car should arrive at Micah's house tomorrow evening. My SUV being loaded and shipped has reality setting in. And my nerves zapping like live wires.

This is really happening. I am going home.

Gavin: Car with three boxes inside should be at your place tomorrow night.
Micah: Cool. I'll let you know when it arrives. What time is your flight tomorrow?
Gavin: 10am, with a stop in Houston. Should be in Tampa between 7-7:30pm.

Micah: If your shit arrives before you land, want me to pick you up?

Gavin: Nah. I'll just grab an Uber.

Micah: See you tomorrow. Tell your mom I said hi. Fly safe.

After my car is driven off, I go back in the house that no longer belongs to me and breathe deeply. In Los Angeles, houses sell faster than imaginable. At least that is what my realtor said. Regardless of the reason, I am happy to have things coming together. Call it divine intervention or luck of the draw—I don't care—but thank god I was able to check every item off my to-do list.

Scanning the empty house, I sigh. The day I put my house on the market, I also asked every person I knew if they wanted to purchase any of my furniture. A few hours ago, the last piece—my bed—was picked up. With not much furniture in the first place, it wasn't challenging to sell a bed with two nightstands, a couch, loveseat, coffee table, and a dining set. I had buyers lined up on the first day. In less than half a day, each piece was claimed.

Everything kept falling into place. And after each domino fell, I thanked the higher power watching over me. Because obviously someone out there wanted me to repair our broken relationship.

My phone buzzes in my palm, Mom's name and picture flashing on the screen.

"Hey, Mom."

"You ready, honey?"

"Yeah, I just have a couple more boxes for your garage." Yesterday, I took over the majority of what I planned to keep. All I had left was my carry-on for the plane and two small boxes.

"Okay. I'm leaving the house now. We can grab something to eat after I pick you up. See you soon."

"See you soon."

Mom and I sit in silence at the dining room table with two open pizza boxes between us. Of all the things to have for dinner on my last night here, Mom suggested our favorite pizza place. Honestly, it didn't matter what we ate. As long as we spent this time together, I was happy. And as much as I dislike California, I will miss Mom terribly.

"I wish you would come back to Florida with me," I tell her.

She sighs before taking a bite of pizza. After she finishes chewing, she says, "Gavin, maybe I will return in the future. But for now, my place is here. Maybe I'll feel different once you're gone, but I won't know until that happens."

I nod, accepting her answer. "Just hate that you'll be out here alone. If Dad was still alive, I'd feel different."

"I'm not alone, Gavin. Believe it or not, I have friends. Lots of them. And we spend time with one another." Mom points her slice of pizza at me and laughs. "Just because I'm a mother and older, doesn't mean I forgot how to enjoy life."

"Ha ha. Fine, I guess I believe you'll make it without me here. But if anything changes…"

"I promise you'll be the first to know."

We finish eating and put the extra pizza in the fridge. Plopping down on the couch, we spend the next two hours laughing at old episodes of *The Simpsons*. The night is the perfect end to my time in Los Angeles. Next to my mom, laughing and spending time together.

And right then, I send a wish to the universe that Mom will want to move back to Florida soon. Because I need her just as much as I do Cora. The only women in my life that matter. The only women who keep me whole and in check. My secret request is selfish, but I don't care. There are some things in life worth being selfish over. Like love.

We rise from the couch around ten thirty, give each other a hug, and head to our respective rooms. I kick off my shoes and tug my shirt over my head before landing on the bed. I stare at the ceiling for a while, counting the plastic, glow-in-the-dark stars I stuck to the ceiling when we first moved here. The stars were a constant reminder of Cora and the French sentiment I once told her. She truly is the stars to my moon. And she illuminates every-thing important in the world. Everything important to me.

And soon, very soon, I will be near her again. See her again. Breathe her in again. Touch her again. Because we haven't reached the end of our road. Not by a long shot. Anyone who tells me otherwise is a fool.

Shortly after I turn off the lamp, I fall asleep under the same stars I did almost thirteen years ago. Stars that spark my mind to dream of the most beautiful woman. The woman I love. The woman I have to win back. No matter what it takes.

When I wake in the morning, Mom is in the kitchen cooking us breakfast. As I sit at the breakfast bar, she slides a plate of eggs, sausage, and toast in front of me. The last woman to make me breakfast was Cora. And I laugh, remembering my first taste of meatless sausage.

"What's so funny?" Mom asks.

I share my story with her and she laughs too. So many things have changed over the years, yet one thing remains the same and true. My love for Cora. And no matter how much has changed for either of us, I will love her regardless.

Mom and I finish breakfast, then talk about my new

agent and how I plan to stay with Micah until I buy a new house. I help her with the dishes and then we prepare to leave. The drive to the airport goes faster than usual. Before realization sets in, Mom and I hug at the departure drop-off. After someone honks their horn, we break apart.

"Call me when you land, please."

"I will, Mom. I love you."

"I love you too, honey." For a moment, I stand rooted in place and stare as her car exits the airport drop-off.

This is it. The day I have been waiting for. Today, I am going home.

One of the hardest things I have ever done is sit on my ass and do nothing. Literally, nothing. Especially when I could be out there, trying to win back the love of my life.

But somehow, Micah has convinced me to sit in his house and be patient. To bide my time. The only thing keeping me sane is searching the internet for houses. Several nice houses have sparked my attention, but none of them give me a sense of fulfillment. And I think the reason is Cora.

If I buy a new home, I want Cora to be a part of the process. To hear her opinions on the appearance—inside and out. Get her input on which kitchen she likes better. If the house gets enough light or has the right number of trees. Or maybe which house she pictures us growing old in together. Which house she imagines us raising children and grandchildren in, their little feet trampling through a large back yard and playing on swings.

I slap my laptop shut and stop staring at houses. No matter what I do to occupy my time, every piece of my life always circles back to Cora. She is literally in every thought I own—awake and asleep.

Turning on the television, I search for something to watch. When I scroll through the guide and see *Lord of the Rings*, I laugh. If the cosmos aren't trying to tell me something, I don't understand what the hell is happening. One sign after another pops up. From the second I decided to mend my mistakes and our past, fortune has been on my side. And after seeing this, I vow to not spend another day sitting on this couch, bored out of my skull, doing nothing.

Just as I start watching the movie, Micah bursts through the front door. "Guess what?" he asks, a little out of breath.

"Whatever you're dying to tell me must be good if you're out of breath."

Micah flips me off. "Well, I was about to give you the

best news since your return yesterday, but now I think I'll wait." He cocks his head and smirks.

Fucker.

"Don't be a dick. I'm sorry if I hurt your feelings." I frown at him for a half second, but the sarcasm doesn't go unnoticed. "What were you going to say?"

He stares at me a minute, tapping a finger against his lips. "A little birdie told me a specific photographer will be out and about tomorrow, taking photos."

At his words, I fly off the couch and grab his face. Practically throttling his skull off his spine. "Where? Tell me where." My voice frantic while my body sings.

"Ah, ah, ah. Not so fast. Tit for tat, my friend." Micah waggles his finger in front of my face.

I drop my hands from his face. "What could I possibly do for you?" At this point, I would do just about anything to see Cora again. Sitting in this house is making me nutty.

"How about you just owe me one in the future? Deal?" Micah asks.

Definitely a deal I can't pass up. "Deal," I say. Micah extends his hand and we shake on it.

A minute later, Micah shares with me all the details Shelly told him about Cora's shoot tomorrow. Shelly knows I have been back in town since yesterday, but Micah asked her to not make Cora aware. But by Shelly knowing I returned home, she and Micah have been secret go-betweens for me. Their sibling bond has never been better and I love how much they are team Gavin-and-Cora-together-again.

Later, when I try to fall asleep on the couch, I spend an hour planning how I will surprise Cora. I have it all mapped out in my head. But the hidden weight in my wallet makes me second-guess what might go down.

My only hope is she doesn't run the opposite direction.

I PARK my car along Central Avenue, near Fifth Street. After I feed the parking meter, I walk into the nearest coffee shop and order a coconut milk latte.

After I'm slightly caffeinated, I wander for a few blocks. I take in all the sights, categorizing what would be great to photograph. Murals on select buildings. Downtown life. Restaurants and museums and shops to visit. The Sundial. The historical Vinoy hotel. Tampa Bay, from the St. Petersburg side. And that's only downtown. I have dates scheduled to shoot other parts of the city.

Once I make it back to my car, I have over ten different sections of downtown St. Petersburg I plan to photograph. I grab my cameras from the back of my car and head toward the farthest location. As I stroll through the morning crowd, I glance over my shoulder a time or two. Every other storefront, I get this odd feeling someone is following me. Like my intuition is having a light bulb moment. But each time I check, I spot no familiar faces in the crowd.

Starting at First Street, I snap photo after photo. A restaurant here, another there. One storefront after another. Downtown has so many unique shops, it is difficult to choose what to photograph. So, I snap as many as possible. Once I go through the editing process, I will siphon out what stays and what goes.

The closer I get to my car, the more it feels as if someone is following me again. So instead of being obvious and staring up and down the street, I step inside a cafe and order a drink.

Once the young girl behind the counter hands me the drink, I sit one table away from the window and stare outside. Girlfriends flock into shops together, smiling and laughing. A man with a little girl on his shoulders walks by. Minutes pass and I recognize no one on the sidewalk, but the twinge in my gut remains.

Five steps from opening the door, I spot him. Gavin.

He stands across the street, in front of a clothing store, watching me. How long has he been there? Why wasn't I checking across the street too? Clad in a pair of dark gray and black checkered shorts, a form-fitting black T-shirt, and dark sunglasses shielding his eyes.

I don't need to see his eyes to know he has missed just as much sleep as me. Has been in just as much pain as I have been.

We stand staring at one another for a moment. And it isn't until someone else leaves the cafe that I move from where I have been locked in place. As my feet shuffle toward the exit, he raises his hand and waves.

When I step onto the sidewalk, I shift to the side and move out of pedestrian foot traffic. The moment I lock eyes with Gavin again, he starts crossing the street and walking in my direction. When he crosses the double line in the center of the street, I run. And I hear him yelling and running after me.

"Cora!" Gavin screams. "Cora, wait!"

With my arms pinning the cameras to my chest, my run morphs into an awkward jog. I weave in and out of the growing crowd, spotting my car in the spaces one block away.

I will make it before he catches me.

Repeating the mantra with my eyes focused on the driver's side door of my car, I almost jog in front of a moving car. Almost. But Gavin yanks on my bicep just in time to pull me out of the street.

"Oh my god, Cora! Are you okay?" Gavin holds me at arm's length and inspects me head to toe. Once he determines I am unscathed and his breathing settles enough, he speaks up. "You didn't have to run into traffic to get away from me."

Stunned, I stare back at him. Is he really here? Is he back? For good? I shake my head, not wanting to get ahead of myself. One step at a time, Cora. No sense in getting your hopes up when you don't have all the facts.

"I wasn't purposely running into traffic. Just wasn't paying attention. Sorry I scared you," I say. Because it's true. I would never do anything to that extreme.

Gavin bends at the waist, places his hands on his knees and breathes heavily. After a moment, his breathing regulates and he stands up straight. "Why were you running from me?" He studies the lines of my face as his bunch just above the bridge of his nose.

"Don't know. Guess I thought it'd be better than confronting you and losing my shit. The last few weeks have been a clusterfuck. Not sure how much more I can handle," I admit.

He nods and purses his lips before relaxing them again. "I deserve that. Can we please go somewhere and talk? There's a lot I need to tell you. And even more wrongs I need to make right." He shoves his hands in his pockets and teeters back on his heels as he regards me.

We silently stand on the sidewalk for a couple awkward moments while I weigh my options. If I don't grant him time to get everything out in the open, he will continue to pursue me tomorrow and every day thereafter. Plus, I need to know where everything stands with his agent and *her*. And where we stand. But where we stand will depend on what he tells me.

I would like to believe I am capable of forgiving him for the lies. Because deep down, he didn't do it with the intention of hurting me. He simply thought it was something he could resolve without issue.

Only time will tell.

"Yes. Let's find somewhere to get lunch. Then you can tell me whatever it is you need to. But I make no promises about how I'll feel afterward."

He nods. "I accept that. If I were you, I'd feel the same."

Gavin and I walk to my car and I stow my cameras. A few minutes later, we stroll into the Cider Press Cafe and get seated near the window. I peek at him over my menu, waiting to see his expression as he reads the food options. As soon as his gray irises thin and pupils dilate, I laugh. At least eating here will lighten the mood as we discuss some heavy stuff. Because right now, I need a good laugh more than anything.

Eleven years ago

I STAND in a sea of suffocating black polyester. Bodies bump against me every five seconds, and the lack of personal space pisses me off. Who the hell organized this damn function? Whoever the fucker is, they should be fired. Because this is nothing short of chaos.

After a few minutes, we are all corralled through a doorway and led out to a spread of plastic folding chairs facing a stage. On the stage is a podium, a table, and several more folding chairs. The principal and other school staff sit on the stage chairs, their robes puffy and sashes colorful. A person stands in the aisle along the student seating, directing us to which row we're to sit in. Not like it matters, we all have our names written on a card that we hand to someone to read.

Once we are all seated, various teachers stand at the podium and share positive words for the future. I choose to ignore their words. The only reason I agreed to do this whole ceremony bullshit is the end result I hope to receive. A trip home to Florida.

The ceremony passes with nothing monumental occurring. When it ends, I walk into a room where we get our actual diploma. The second it is in my hands, elation courses through me. This small rectangle of paper is my ticket back to Cora. My ticket home.

Although we haven't spoken in close to two years, I hope she will forgive me. When I stopped answering her letters, calls and texts, my intention was to do what was best for her, since I had no way to see her. To let her go.

But after that letter and those drawings she sent me, I am nervous as hell about how she will react to seeing me again. I went about things a shitty way, but what else was I supposed to do? We were in a fucked-up situation and I thought what I was doing would mend it all somehow.

But I was wrong. Dead wrong.

I walk out of the back and go in search of my parents. They stand outside, waiting for me with giant smiles plastered on their faces. After a handful of photos are taken, we head to the car and drive to a restaurant for my graduation dinner. In the car, they reminisce over the ceremony and how nice it was. I stare out the window and pray it won't be much longer before I don't see this skyline again.

Once we order food and my parents express their unwavering excitement, I mentally prepare to ask the question I have been waiting to ask for the past two years. Asking is going to burst the joy bubble they are trapped in, but I don't care. My bubble hasn't held joy since I was forced to leave Florida and step foot in this state.

"Mom? Dad? Can we talk about me moving back to Florida?" Straight forward and to the point. No need to beat around the bush. A man on a mission.

Mom tips her head to the side as a frown takes residence on her lips. Dad doesn't move, his expression stoic. Their lack of communication says more than any words ever will. The silence tells me the trip I have longed to make won't be happening. But I refuse to believe it until I hear the actual words. Until they tell me I cannot go.

"Gavin—" Mom starts, but pauses to look at Dad for silent support "—I would love nothing more than for you to be where you want to be. But things have been really tight for us financially. And right now, we just don't have the money to fly you to Florida."

I fucking knew this would happen. Knew it. As soon as we got here, I should have gone to every store and restaurant and applied for a job. Bagboy, stocker, cashier, busboy. Anything. If I had, maybe I would have more than enough money by now to leave. But I was so wrapped up in throwing a pity party for myself, I didn't do shit.

Fuck my life.

"So there's nothing we can do? Didn't you have some college fund for me? If so, cash it in. I have zero plans to go to college, especially here."

"Son, I wish it were that simple," Dad chimes in. "We did have a college fund for you, but we had to cash it in shortly after we moved here. Things have been a little tougher than we suspected. I'm sorry."

You have got to be fucking kidding me. Not only can I not go back to Florida, but college isn't even an option. I may not have wanted to attend college, but they banked on my not mentioning it. Score one for the parentals. Zero for the child. Fucking bullshit.

"Wow. I don't know how to respond to any of this. You both knew my plans after graduation. How could you not say anything to me? You could've suggested I go out and get a job. If only for three or four months. At least I'd have money to fly home."

"This is home, Gavin," Mom says.

"This has never been home, Mom. You know it just as much as I do," I snap.

"Don't speak that way to your mother," Dad states, his voice sharp and stern. "We have had to make tough decisions for our family and I wouldn't change a single one. You may not have liked our choices. You may not like your life here. But you *will* respect us."

Wow. Just wow. So does respect only go one way? The parents *deserve* it, but their children don't? What sort of asinine bullshit is that? Yes, I was underage when we moved and didn't have a say in the matter. I accept it. But to purposely hide this… I am done.

"Sorry, Mom. Sorry, Dad," I seethe. "I respect you. This just fucking sucks! And I can't help but wonder why neither of you said a damn word to me sooner. Oh, I know," I say, holding up a finger and firmly pressing my lips together. "Because you knew this would be my reaction, that's why. Fucking bullshit."

"Watch your mouth, Gavin," Dad snaps.

I shake my head. "It's a little late for that, Dad. You forget, I'm an adult. Like you never swore when you were younger."

Mom and Dad go silent on the opposite side of the table, shutting down the conversation. Our server delivers the food a minute later, but I don't eat a bite. Instead, I open up the photos on my phone and scroll through the folder marked "C+G." With each swipe, my throat swells and the back of my eyes sting.

Fuck.

There is one singular thing I have wanted for the last two years. One thing that provided purpose and gave me hope. To go home to Cora. To see her beautiful face cupped between my hands again. Listen to her laughter as I tickle her in that spot under her ribs only I know about. Wrap my arms around her waist and draw her close to my body as we lay on the couch and watch *Lord of the Rings* for the hundredth time.

But now it seems that won't be happening. Not unless I figure out how to get there on my own. And it looks as though that is my only option. But I will make it happen.

My fourth job interview ends like the previous three. With a *"we'll get back to you soon."* Which equals we have no intention of hiring you. Why is it so fucking hard to get a job? Working retail isn't rocket science.

I walk out of the preppy clothing store with my head hung low. *Where the hell will I get a job?* At this point, I am not above selling shit on the streets to get the money I need. Whatever it takes to get me back to Cora. And although I haven't spoken with her in far too long, in my mind's eye, I picture her face lighting up the moment we reconnect. As if we scoured the earth to find each other and succeeded.

There is one more interview on my list today. One more opportunity. And I hope like hell it won't end like the last four. This interview is a long shot, but I have to try. At this point, what do I have to lose?

Two hours later, I walk through the front door of Elite Models. My stomach twists in a knot and a bead of sweat rolls down the back of my neck. When I approach the reception desk, a woman ten years my senior gawks at me head to toe. Her perusal isn't distasteful, but makes me want to curl inward.

"Can I help you?"

I step closer to the counter. "Yes. I have an interview with Sharon and Gus."

The woman peels her eyes away from me and scans her computer screen. A few scrolls and clicks later, she locates whatever she had been looking for and smiles. Her fingers tap the keyboard before she picks up the phone and dials.

"Your next candidate is here," she says. Her eyes pop back to my body and visually rip away my clothes. The act is a total violation and I wonder if this is what girls feel like when men ogle them in public. If so, it is awful and makes me want to cover myself with my arms.

She sets the handset back down, but keeps her eyes trained on me. I want to look away, escape the unease of her gaze, but choose not to. Because who knows how she will visually obsess over me when I turn away.

God, this is awkward.

A set of smoky glass doors open and a man walks out. He could be Dad's age, maybe older, but is layered in makeup and trendy clothes that shave years off his appearance. His hair is styled like a magazine ad—not a single strand out of place. For a moment, inferiority swamps me. *I can't do this.* But I have to do this. Every other option has been tossed away.

"Gavin Hunt?" the trendy man asks and I nod. "Hello, Gavin. Gus." He extends a hand and I shake it. "It's nice to meet you. If you'll follow me, we'll get started."

I follow him through the smoky doors. With each step, I ask myself if doing this is the right thing. If getting sucked into the limelight is how I get back to Cora. The hall we walk down is littered with countless photos. Women, men, people my age, people my parents' age. The images range from luxurious to hobo and everything in between. Each face is beautifully sculpted and emotionally connecting with the onlooker.

How the hell do they do that? How the hell would *I* do that?

There is no way I can do this.

Two hours later, I shake Sharon and Gus's hands. They don't throw me the infamous line I have heard at every other interview. Instead, they tell me what time to return on Monday. Relief courses through my veins.

Finally, an opportunity.

Not only did I land a job. I landed the opportunity of a lifetime. Modeling will not only flood my pockets, it will have me back in Cora's arms sooner than expected.

Today ends on a high note and I wish I could share the news with the one person who matters.

Soon. After I get a couple photo shoots under my belt, I will call Cora and let her know the good news. That I will return home.

Why is this shit so goddamn difficult?

Every photo I have studied makes modeling seem effortless. Smiles and smirks and deadpan expressions. All in my repertoire. Stand in front of the camera, plaster your face with whatever emotion the photographer seeks and pose. Boom. Photo acquired.

Wrong.

After several failed attempts to appear smoldering, I am asked to put my shirt back on and report to Karen on the third floor. What the fuck is smoldering anyway? If I didn't fear the repercussions of having my phone out, I would search the term online.

Instead, now I sit in a room with five other people. Our chairs in a small circle facing each other. Feels like I am at a group therapy session. My knee bounces and I gnaw on my thumbnail.

A fifty-something woman glides into the room. Yes,

glides. For a moment, I wonder if she wears special shoes under her floor-length, flowy dress. She owns the room in one breath. Everyone in the circle equally mesmerized by her appearance. Her finesse. Her ability to instantly garner everyone's attention.

"Good afternoon. I'm Karen, your modeling coach."

Modeling coach? Damnit. Obviously, my modeling skills were zero on a scale of a million. Because this sounds like school. And school hasn't been something I excelled in since moving.

The girl beside me leans in close. "Is it just me? Does this lady make you feel as inadequate as she does me?"

I lean an inch away and glance at her a moment. "Uh, I guess." I shrug. Inadequate wasn't quite the word I would choose. Maybe intimidated.

The girl smiles big at me. Her smile makes me more uncomfortable than Karen's entrance and presence. Not able to pinpoint my discomfort, I opt for niceties and extend my hand to her.

"Hi, I'm Gavin."

She stares at my hand a moment, a few emotions flit across her face but don't linger. Then she takes my hand and shakes it. "Layla." Her eyes ping to mine and she keeps our hands connected. I want to yank it back. Her touch scalds my skin. Not in the way Cora's touch heats every molecule inside me. Rather, Layla's skin on mine is invasive. Parasitic. Wrong.

When she doesn't remove her hand from mine after

an uncomfortable five breaths, I slip mine away. The second she looks away from me, I wipe my hand on my jeans. Something about this girl makes me uneasy. The only person I read easily was Cora. So, it confounds me to not figure out why this girl makes me uneasy.

Maybe she is just as upset about being in this class as I am. Maybe she is only trying to be friendly.

I lean back in my chair and listen to Karen prattle on about why we are all here. Honestly, if this class makes me better at modeling, I am all for it. It gets me one more step closer to Cora. The main reason I'm doing this in the first place.

For her. For us. And our future.

Hours later, the class ends. All of us numb from the lessons on facial expressions and how to achieve them. According to Karen, we will be seeing her five days a week for the foreseeable future. Once she determines we are worthy of "graduating," she will pass such information to the appropriate people.

In other words, it may be weeks or months before I model. Weeks or months before I take a decent photo. Weeks or months before I earn a penny.

On the upside, the modeling agency pays for the classes. Only because we are "assets." Calling me an asset is objectifying, but I suck it up. Modeling is just temporary. A stepping stone to get me where I need to be.

As I leave for the day, Layla stops me. "Hey, Gavin.

You want to grab something to eat? I could eat a cow after today." She laughs and it sounds forced. Awkward. Exaggerated.

All I want is to go home and crash. But it would be nice to know someone else in this boat. Someone I can talk to when I have a rough day. A friend. "Yeah, sure."

The moment I agree, a rock plummets in my gut. It sinks and settles deep. Nausea threatens and I shove it down. Layla is a nice person—at least that is what I continually tell myself. Our relationship will only consist of friendship. Nothing more.

No one will ever take Cora's place. No one.

Present

THE SERVER WALKS AWAY and I wonder what the hell I just ordered. Some mock version of pulled "pork." Except this place serves no meat. Cora assures me it was a good choice, but I will be the judge.

Cora picks up her water and sips it while staring out the window. Her fingers twist and roll the paper straw while her eyes narrow slightly then go back to their normal shape. Occasionally, she bites the inside of her cheek. Beneath the table, her leg bounces and ghosts against mine every other breath.

Does she feel it each time her skin grazes mine? She is so lost in her thoughts, I doubt it. But I do. Every. Single. Time.

"Cora."

Her eyes dart from the window to mine as she snaps out of her fog. "Huh?"

"Why are you so nervous?"

She rolls her eyes and it is fucking adorable. "Don't be silly, Gavin. I'm not nervous." Her leg bounces faster.

I tilt my head and study her a minute. "You know you can't fool me. So why try?"

Cora huffs and sets her water down. A second later, she tucks her hands under her thighs. We sit in silence a moment, staring at each other. Holding her gaze has never been uncomfortable, whether for five seconds or five minutes.

And then I remember the reason why we are sitting together right now. The reason she's giving me a chance. Because she is waiting to hear my truth. A truth I swore to tell her. That I plan to tell her. I only hope she listens. Truly listens and digests what I say.

"I'm sorry," I say. An apology is the best place to start. Unfortunately, I have far too much to apologize for.

Her leg finally stops bouncing. "Sorry? And what exactly are you sorry for?" Her question slaps me in the face. A slap I more than deserve. A slap I will take like a man.

I reach under the table and rest a hand on her knee. The simple and innocent touch soothes my nervousness and helps me focus. "Where do I begin?" I pause a moment to gather my thoughts. She needs to know everything, but I don't want to bounce from one end to the other and back again.

My question was meant to be rhetorical, but she answers. "How about the beginning. I find that to always be the best place."

Cora's snappy demeanor has me on the cusp of smiling. On the verge of teasing and light sarcasm. But the last thing I need is to piss her off more, so I resist the urge and trudge forward.

"I'm sorry I stopped answering your calls and texts. Sorry I didn't return a single one of them. My parents had thrown every hope I had of getting back to you out the window. So, I thought I was doing the right thing by letting you go. By giving you a chance to move on without me. To have a life and smile and maybe find love again."

A glutton for punishment, I refuse to look away from her. Refuse to not see every emotion she feels as my words set in. As I share the reason why I abandoned her years ago. Even as her eyes brim red and well in the corners. Even as her brow furrows and lips purse. She breaks eye contact and shifts her gaze to the street, not looking at anything specific. She just has difficulty looking at me. A tear rolls down her cheek and she swipes it away with the back of her hand. Her chin quivers as she clamps her lips between her teeth.

I walked into this knowing sour memories would be rehashed. That me spilling my truth, telling her where my head was at, would be hard to hear. But fuck, it hurts to watch her break down in front of me. To see her fighting off emotions as we sit in public and talk about the most painful parts of our past.

After a minute, I give her knee a squeeze. Her soft green bloodshot eyes come back to mine and the emotion in them is raw. It claws at my heart and shreds it in a million pieces. As painful as this is, I did this to her. And I deserve every gut-wrenching second of the pain I feel. Her pain.

"Why didn't you tell me?" she croaks out. "Why didn't you call or text or write and tell me what was happening? We shared everything with each other. Everything." She shakes her head. "But you up and decided to make this monumental decision without me." She sucks in a breath and speaks on the exhale. "Gavin, I shut down. Detached from the world and crawled into a hole. All I wanted was to talk with you. My best friend. My everything. And you shut me out."

A fist wraps around my heart and constricts the organ like a squeaky toy. Over and over and over.

How could I have been such a dick? How could I have been so selfish? Everything I did was in the hopes of Cora not being in pain. At least that's what I kept telling myself. I thought letting her go was the best option. What other option was there? I had no way to get to her, and my parents did nothing to help. So, in my eyes, letting her live life without restriction seemed like the better option. I didn't want her to feel obligated—to me or the possibility of me.

Obviously, I am a fucking idiot.

"No matter what I say, it'll never make up for what I did. But I'd like to try now. Try to fix what I've done. Will you let me try? Please."

I reach for my wallet and she follows my every move. Behind my license, I retrieve a folded piece of yellowing paper with tattered edges. After a deep breath, I set it on the table and slide it to her.

Cora's red-rimmed eyes study my face. Her eyes dart between mine. Her lips press in a firm line and wobble side to side. And her chin continues to tremor as she reaches for the paper. Fixing this is not enough. I need to make it up to her every day of forever. And I will. I swear I will.

She sniffles and nods. "You know I will. But you have to tell me everything. No more secrets." She holds up the paper. "What's this?"

Before I answer, the server delivers our food to the table and cuts off our conversation. Cora tucks the paper in her pocket and I know she will read it when she is alone. Read the last letter she sent me, smudged with her tears and mine.

I stare down at the basket. I have no clue what I am about to eat, but I pick it up and bite down. An odd texture licks my tongue, but tastes weirdly like pulled pork. I shrug and continue eating while Cora giggles across from me. At least my eating brings a smile to her face. A smile is a smile, and I will call it a step in the right direction.

A few minutes pass before I wipe my hands clean and lean back in my chair. "I sold my house in California. Currently, I'm sleeping on Micah's couch until I find my own place."

Cora sits quietly across from me. Questions flit over her face, but she doesn't ask a single one. Her mouth opens and closes. This happens a few times before she finally speaks. "Oh. What about your mom?"

I love how she worries about my mom, now that I moved away. "She'll be okay. I think she was surprised it took me so long to move back. We argued so much the first two years out there. She expected me to run away and hitchhike back to Florida." The idea was given serious merit, but was ignored after the reality of how far I *wouldn't* get settled.

Cora nods and I continue. "When I got back to California, I sat down with Mom and discussed my plan to move back. Told her about the photo shoot with you. Also told her my time out west should have ended years ago. She was more than understanding and offered to help me in any way possible."

"I miss your mom," Cora says.

I lean forward and lay my hand on her knee under the table again. "She misses you, too. I wouldn't be surprised if she visits soon, now that I've moved away.

She'll probably wait until I have a place." I sip my water, allowing a few breaths to pass before I speak again. "Alyson and Layla have been dealt with also."

I don't miss the way Cora flinches when I say Layla's name. The way her lips curl for a split second. But she collects herself and responds as if she had no reaction. "Uh, I'm not sure what to say."

"There's nothing to say. I'm only sorry you were on the receiving end of their jealousy. The moment I got back to California, I reviewed my contracts and sought out a new agent. After I finished my final shoot with Layla, I fired Alyson and told Layla I never wanted to see or hear from her again. It went about as smooth as expected."

"Gavin, you didn't have to do that. Not for me."

Although her words tell me I didn't need to make such a drastic change in my life, I don't miss the way her body sags in relief. The small shift in her demeanor speaks a thousand words her lips won't. Ease slips into her expression and I know what I did was the first step in the right direction.

"Yes, I did. But not just for you, I did it for myself also. Too many nights have passed since I set out to come back to you. When I started modeling, it was to earn as much money as possible so I could fly back to Florida. To you. I hadn't spoken to you in over a year, but not a day went by where my goal changed. Being with you has always been my endgame."

She scoots back in her seat and her knee shifts out of my reach. Her elbows rest on the table as she lays her forearms toward me. Palms up, her hands rest as an open invitation for mine. As eager as I am to lay my hands on hers, to feel her warmth, to connect with her intimately, I don't rush this. I slowly withdraw my hands from under the table and place them in hers. Beneath my palms, her fingers trace steady lines along my skin.

I close my eyes and surrender to my senses. How her soft skin faintly brushes my palms as she trails her fingertips there. Subtle hints of her frankincense and gardenia scent wisp in the air and flutter in my nose. A small hitch in her breathing as she continues to reconnect a bond once severed. The shiver down my spine and fast-growing bloom of heat in my chest as it all swirls together.

God, I want to kiss her. More than anything.

When my eyes reopen, Cora sits across from me slack-jawed. So fucking beautiful.

No matter how much time has passed, she is still the only woman I see. The only woman I want beside me. Today and every day that follows. Cora is it for me. And I assume the same holds true for her. Because she has never moved on from us either. Not fully.

"Gavin, how did *she* go from being your friend to your fiancée?" I don't miss the way Cora says *she* with distaste on her tongue. But I don't blame her. No doubt I would feel equally as disgusted if the situation were reversed.

"Layla wasn't getting as many callbacks or opportunities for shoots. My career, on the other hand, was booming. Alyson sat down with the two of us and threw out the idea of us "being engaged." Of course, it would be strictly for publicity reasons, but I still wasn't keen. Alyson said we would cut it short after Layla was seen enough times with me. But every time I brought it up, Alyson told me to wait another month. That some brand was on the fence of signing Layla. And I obviously bought the lie every time. From the get-go, something didn't sit right with me when it came to Layla, but I ignored it. I'll never be so naïve again."

I curl my fingers into hers and stare at our hands a moment. The reality of my naïveté is a punch to the gut. How much time was stolen from me because of it? Countless months and years. All because I had tunnel vision—Cora standing in the light at the end. Alyson and Layla—both who knew about the woman in Florida, but not who she was—took advantage of me. Of my eagerness to return to her. They played me. And I had been the damn fool falling for every line and promise.

"After my last shoot, I had an interview scheduled with The Heart of Hollywood. Millions of eyes would see or hear my interview. I blasted the truth to everyone. About Alyson and Layla. How my engagement was a ruse to garner attention for Layla and her lackluster modeling career. And then I told millions of people about you. About us. How I ran into the love of my life and instantly decided I was moving home."

Across from me, Cora gasps. For a completely different reason, her eyes pool, soften. Her lips tremble. And I can't take it anymore. No longer able to stay on the opposite side of the table, I rise and slide into the seat beside her. She watches my every move as she bites her lower lip.

"Gavin," she whispers.

I frame her face with my hands and brush away a fallen tear. Leaning into her, my lips a breath from hers, I tell Cora the words only meant for her.

"I love you. Only you. Always."

And as badly as I want to kiss her, I resist the urge. With all the shit I have put Cora through, I won't fuck this up. I want her to want to kiss me. Want her to initiate. Need her to be the one who moves us forward. No matter what, my heart is hers. Always has been. Always will be. But I crushed her heart all those years ago. And I will wait however long it takes for her to be ready for us. For me.

Cora wraps her hands around my forearms and grips them like it's her last breath. Her gaze unwavering as her watery green eyes stare up at me. "I love you, too." She pinches her eyes shut and wetness slips between her lashes to my fingertips. I wipe them away, then lift my lips to her lids and kiss them each with reverence.

"I know it will take time, but I vow to make us whole again. Whatever I need to do to fix us, I will. Without you, nothing else matters."

She attempts to nod, but my hands keep her face hostage. We both laugh a moment, and I am certain we look like lunatics. But as long as Cora is with me, I don't give a damn what people think of me. With her by my side, I can be anyone.

After I drop my hands, I switch to a more serious tone. "Go out with me. On a date. Please?"

Cora reaches up and cups my cheeks, scratching my jawline before her hands fall to my chest and rest over my heart. "What if we go out with everyone? Obviously, you know Micah and Shelly, but I would love for you to get to know Jonas and Erin better. They've been there for me when I needed them. They're family. And I really want you to be comfortable with them."

Hanging out with everyone else isn't exactly what I had in mind for a date with Cora, but I will take every moment she grants me. If this is important to her—Jonas and I being friendly—I will set aside my jealousy. Jealousy over the fact that this guy has spent more years with her than I have. Although their relationship is strictly platonic, I am not blind to the way he looks at her. Maybe time with him is the perfect idea. For both of us.

"Okay, let's go out with everyone. When? Where?"

She claps and fidgets in her seat. "Yay! I'll talk to

Shelly and we'll figure everything out. Then you'll be the next to know."

Her happiness is infectious. It lures me in and holds me captive. And I stay willingly, a prisoner of her heart. Whatever it takes to make my girl happy, I plan to do it. Because seeing her smile brightens the darkest skies.

After I pay the bill, we walk back to her car hand in hand. Our stride is leisure. Our voices absent. And it is absolute perfection. When we reach her car, I spin her around and wrap my arms around her. I rest my chin on the crown of her head and gently rock side to side, shutting my eyes and relishing the weight of her body pressed to mine. Her arms snake around my back and squeeze me tight. I don't want to let her go. Not now. Not ever.

I kiss her hair, release my hold on her and run my hands down her biceps. "Call me when you get everything sorted out with Shelly."

She tips her head back and meets my sunglass-covered eyes. "I will. Promise."

I step back and play with a strand of her hair. "I love you. See you soon."

God, I don't want to walk away, but know I need to. Cora needs to have control over what happens with us. What happens next. Unbeknownst to her, I have put my life and the future of us in her hands. My fitful heart and restless soul sit nestled inside her. This time around, she makes all the decisions and I make none.

"I love you, too."

As soon as she says the words, I pivot and walk away. Her eyes singe me as I amble down the sidewalk, away from her and into the unknown. But there is no other place I would rather be.

It FEELS as if I am in grade school again as I stand outside the entrance of Dave and Busters. Bright orange and yellow paint coat the brick exterior. A large, angular metal awning hangs over the entrance. The automatic doors whoosh open then glide shut. The action mesmerizes me briefly until Shelly comes up behind me, bouncing like an adolescent.

What is it about an arcade that makes you feel twenty years younger? Who knows, but whatever it is, I love it.

Shelly unlocks her phone and scrolls through her text history. A moment later, she assures me everyone should be here in the next ten minutes.

We loiter near the entrance, steering clear of patrons coming or going, and get lost in our cell phones. Shelly zones out in social media land while I check my email. A few minutes later, Erin and Jonas walk up.

We are catching up when I spot Micah and Gavin getting out of an all-black Range Rover. Black paint, pitch-black tint, blacked-out logos. All. Black. Although I only see Micah on occasion, I know this car isn't his. This must be Gavin's car. And the idea of him owning an all-black custom vehicle has me smiling like an idiot.

When they approach us, Micah rolls his eyes at me and I laugh. Micah and I will never share best friend status, but we will always be family. Not only because of my friendship with Shelly, but also because of Gavin. Micah will just have to learn to live with me being around. He is the grumpy big brother I never had and I am the annoying little sister he wished he didn't have.

Gavin steps up and encircles me with his arms, kissing the top of my head. A charm of hummingbirds takes flight in my chest, wings fluttering rapidly and stealing my breath. The more Gavin inserts himself back into my life, the less I want to resist him. Part of me recalls the last time we were in this place—inseparable—and what life was like when he left. That part of me keeps the barrier I have built around my heart upright. Solid. Impenetrable.

Or so I keep telling myself.

When I got home from St. Pete and emptied my pockets, the worn paper mocked me for hours. Until I unfolded the creased edges and saw what he gave me. What he had stashed in his wallet. *My letter*. The last letter I wrote him. On our anniversary, six months after he left.

Seeing that letter again stirred up more than a decade's worth of emotions. But the fact he kept it, tucked it in his wallet, said more than words ever would.

He promises to repair every cut and scrape and rift between us. And I believe him. But I need evidence. And until I see the proof with my own eyes, I still can't expose myself fully. Not yet. Not until I have absolute reassurance he will stay.

After we load up our gaming cards and purchase drinks, we wander through the arcade and scope out all the games. Micah heads over to the virtual reality area while Shelly, Erin, and Jonas go toward the classic arcade games. As soon as Shelly decided we were coming here, my first thought was Skee-Ball. Not only was it my favorite arcade game to play. It also happens to be Gavin's favorite.

"Skee-Ball?" Gavin asks. He cocks a brow up in challenge.

"As if you need to ask."

One of our many rendezvous years ago was to a local arcade. We would play Skee-Ball for hours. Not for tickets, but for bragging rights. Gavin won more times than I did. But when I did win, I rubbed it in his face for weeks. Whatever tickets we won, we handed over to children nearby.

Tonight would be no different. Minus the tickets.

I have been here with Shelly and Jonas several times over the years. And I have broken some high score records. Not that I plan to give this statistical information to Gavin. But my Skee-Ball game is strong. So strong, I am willing to bet money he hasn't played since the last time we played together and can add another Skee-Ball trophy to the shelf. Which works great for me.

We step up to the lanes and swipe our cards. I glance over at him and feel a little cocky. "You ready to get your ass handed to you?"

He throws his head back and laughs, his entire frame shaking. "Who's handing it to me? You?"

"Not sure how good your game is, but I've been practicing." I pop an eyebrow and give a snide smile.

"Have you now?" The balls roll down the chute and clunk together. "What makes you think I haven't been practicing?"

I pick up a ball and shrug. "Call it a hunch." Then I face the lane, swing my arm back and release the wooden ball. It rolls up the lane with perfect precision and flies into the 100-point hole. With pride lighting up my face, I face Gavin again and shrug again. "Whatcha got, Hunt?"

"Oh, it's on, baby." Gavin smirks and lines up to shoot the ball. But I zone out. Molecule by molecule, my body comes alive. Warmth blossoms in my chest, spreading its petals open like the roses Gavin sent me. I get lost in the intimacy of this moment. Of his term of endearment for me. In the banter and ease with which we slip into it like second nature. How being beside him feels right on so many levels.

As much as I want to ease into a life with Gavin, it won't happen. Because that is not how things have ever been between us.

From the first day we met, under our tree, we were destined for more. We slipped into friendship easier than anyone else. Our friendship morphing into best friends was inevitable. We loved spending time together and laughed without effort. Everyone said they knew we would start dating. It was only us who didn't see it happening. Not until that day at the beach over Thanksgiving break.

Our first kiss. The most amazing and memorable kiss of my life. The kiss that started it all.

From that moment forward, I never wanted to kiss another person in my life. My body sang for Gavin. Hummed with hunger and lust and love. No one else has lit my soul on fire like Gavin. And no one else ever will. When one person holds the key to your heart, no other key will ever unlock it. Gavin has always been my key.

Watching Gavin beside me, my heart swells like a hot air balloon—hot and combustible. All the old feelings I buried for thirteen years assault me in the middle of the arcade. Hit me like a hammer to the chest and leave me breathless. I want to yell and cry, cheer and sing, throw myself at him and crush him in my arms. He tosses another ball up the lane, oblivious to my never-ending stare down, and scores another forty points. He glances up at my score and notices it hasn't changed since my first roll.

Gavin rotates his head and drops his gaze to mine. "You okay, baby?" There it is again. The familiar endearment I love rolling off his tongue. And the flutters that come along with it.

Fuck. They're coming. The back of my eyes sting as I nod. I swallow down the expanding boulder in my throat and work to answer him. "Yeah, I'm good."

He sets his ball down and steps up to me, running his fingers through my loose strands. "What's wrong?" Bending his knees, he comes eye level with me. "Talk to me."

I swallow again and tip my head back, batting my lashes. *No crying, Cora. No more tears. Not even happy tears.*

"Just remembering us. This." I gesture to the lanes. "How things were before. How comfortable and easy it is to be with you."

He stands tall and peers down at me, his thumb dusting over my bottom lip. "We've always had this effortless connection. Do you know why that is, baby?"

I fear opening my mouth, fear speaking. Afraid my

words will be unintelligible. Garbled. So, I swallow and shake my head.

Gavin presses his palm against my breastbone and locks his steely eyes on mine. "Because I'm here." Then he reaches out, takes my hand, and places it over his heart. Beneath my palm, his heart beats a vicious rhythm. "And you are here. Before we met, we held a piece of each other hostage. It wasn't until we found each other that those pieces reconnected. As if they'd known each other in another lifetime."

I will not fucking cry.

"Cora, you're it for me. No matter how hard I tried to forget about you, no matter what I did over the last thirteen years, you always danced in my dreams and called out to my heart. I may have ignored it for stupid reasons, but it was there nonetheless."

Goddamnit.

He is going to make me cry. He rests his cheek against mine as his lips hover near my ear. My chest rises and falls as I gasp for breath. I pinch my eyes shut. Swallow hard. Curl and uncurl my fingers.

"I love you, Cora. More than anything or anyone in this world. And fuck if I don't want to kiss you in the middle of this arcade, in front of all these people."

My breath comes faster, but I don't say a word. Will he kiss me? I want to kiss him, but still hesitate. Kissing Gavin again will end any chance I have at resistance. We need time. Time to relearn each other. Time to adjust to a newer version of us. A little more time.

Or am I being absurd?

We have spent so much time apart. Days and months and years disconnected. Broken. Hurt. Do I really want to waste more time? Do I really want to keep him at arm's length? No, I don't. And keeping us divided when he has done everything in his power to bring us back together is asinine.

I lean back from Gavin just enough to see his eyes. If I shift an inch to the side, we would kiss. His eyes lock on mine and read every thought passing through them. And I know he knows what I think. He doesn't flinch or veer from his position. A second later, his eyes close and he draws in a labored breath.

This is it. The moment we have been leading up to. The inevitable.

I line my lips up with his, leaving only a shadow between us. Just as I lean in, just as I'm about to give myself over to him, someone brushes my arm and I retreat.

"Hey, man. Sorry to interrupt. Can I talk with you a minute?"

I open my eyes and spot Jonas beside us. His gaze fixed on Gavin, who is staring at me. Gavin's eyes burn with familiar longing. Something I saw every time he looked at me years ago. Something primal and potent and only ours. It resonates in my marrow. Keeps the chambers of my heart beating. Jonas may be inches from us, but we only see each other. Only *feel* each other.

Gavin's eyes still connected with mine, he answers Jonas. "Sure, man. What's up?"

Jonas shifts foot to foot. "Maybe over there." Jonas points to a table ten feet from us.

"Yeah, no problem." Gavin kisses my forehead. "I'll be back in a minute, baby. Finish my game and yours."

I nod and watch as Gavin and Jonas walk over to the empty table and sit down. They sit so neither of them faces me, but I see both their profiles. Jonas starts talking and Gavin listens intently. Seeing as I can't read lips, staring at them will get me nowhere.

So, I go back to the game, tossing ball after ball up my lane and Gavin's. When his game ends, I finish the round on my lane. Occasionally, I peek over my shoulder at them. They don't shift in position. Neither of them appears to be angry or ready to throw down—which is a good sign. Two more rounds pass before Gavin walks back over to me. His expression neutral.

"Hey. What did Jonas want to talk to you about?" I ask.

He wraps his arms around me and squeezes me close. "I'll tell you in a little bit. Are you hungry?" He kisses my forehead then leans back to peer down at me.

I don't argue with him. If Gavin says he will tell me later, he will. "Yeah. Let's find everyone else and grab dinner."

Micah seems a bit perturbed when we disrupt his virtual reality simulation, but agrees to meet us at a table. A moment later, we locate Shelly and Erin playing Dance Dance Revolution—Jonas teasing their dance skills.

We all converge at a table and order drinks and food. Light chatter fills the space between us. The dynamic between Gavin and Jonas has shifted into something unfamiliar. They sit opposite one another, but don't look or speak to each other. I find it very peculiar. I want to ask Gavin what they talked about, but remind myself he will share with me later. So, I ask Shelly and Erin who is winning their DDR showdown.

I never got into DDR. Classic games have always been my thing. Pinball, Skee-Ball, Pac-Man. But I love Shelly and Erin's enthusiasm for DDR. So, like the amazing best friend that I am, I listen as they regale us with colorful accounts of their competitions. And to be honest, they are pretty hardcore. Intimidating. Kind of makes me glad I never got into it.

Micah and Gavin talk quietly beside me. Micah mentions Peyton and I stop listening. It isn't my place to interrupt two guys chatting about a girl. Especially one I don't know. Who knows how much Micah has told Gavin. But if Micah is bringing her up again, one thing is certain. Micah has a major interest in her. Hopefully Gavin can reassure him that it is okay to move on from his ex. She was a real piece of work and it sucks he still harbors feelings for her.

I peer at Jonas and note his eyes glued to me. How long has he been staring? I wiggle in my seat and Gavin places a hand on my thigh. Ease passes through him to me and I relax into his side.

Jonas mouths *you okay?* His eyes pinch at the corners and his lips form a tight line. I smile and nod at him. *Yeah. Perfect.* I mouth back as I rest a hand over Gavin's. Everything is exactly as it should be in this moment. How it should have been for years.

When we finish eating, Jonas, Shelly, and Erin leave. When hugs are exchanged, Jonas whispers in my ear. "Good to see you happy. It suits you."

"Thank you," I whisper back, hugging him a little harder.

Micah tells us he will be back after another game and then be ready to leave. After Micah walks off, I ask Gavin what he and Jonas talked about earlier.

"Jonas was quite forthcoming." Gavin takes my hand and weaves his fingers with mine. "He told me he's been in love with you for years. We spent most of the conversation getting to know more about each other. And now, I know he's a good guy. I also know he won't be more than your friend because he doesn't want to hurt or lose you." Gavin pauses a moment and chuckles. "He also told me if I ever hurt you again, he'd cut my dick off."

"Oh my god," I say, slapping a hand over my mouth.

"Yeah. At least I know he'll protect you if I'm unable to." Gavin lifts my hand to his lips and presses a few soft kisses to my knuckles. Warmth spreads up my limb, weaves its way through my chest and strikes my heart like lightning. "He also wished us luck. Said this, minus the last couple of weeks, is the happiest he's ever seen you. And that's all he wants."

I swear the guys in my life are out to make me cry. There will always be something I love about Jonas. My love for him is more familial, but love nonetheless. How the hell did I get so lucky? How did I end up with so many wonderful people in my life? Family and friends and people I don't want to live a day without.

"Well it sounds like you two had a great talk." And it sounds like they built a bridge and are trying to meet in the middle for me. I hope one day Gavin and Jonas will be good friends. After time passes, I picture them laughing over beers together.

When Micah finishes his game, we decide to leave. We wander through the parking lot and over to my car. Gavin hands his keys to Micah. "I'll be there in a minute." Micah nods and leaves us. We stare after him as he walks to the Range Rover masked in the shadows.

Once Micah slips into the SUV, Gavin takes a strand of my hair between his fingers and plays with it. "Go on a date with me, baby. Just the two of us."

Every muscle in my body screams at me to say yes. But the wall around my heart stands firmly in place and says we need a little more time before it is just the two of us.

Earlier, I almost annihilated that wall by kissing him, but life intervened. And that little disruption made me wonder if it was a sign I was moving forward too fast. Can't be sure. If Gavin loves me, he won't mind if I tell him to have a little more patience. After all, he had the patience of a saint while we were together.

"Don't hate me," I say as I squint. "Is it okay if we hang with everyone again tomorrow night?"

Please be good with this. Please, please, please.

He strokes my hair, grazes his thumb along my jawline, then kisses the tip of my nose. "If that's what you want, baby. As long as I get to spend time with you, I'm happy."

I sag into his touch. "Thank you."

He kisses the crown of my head then hugs me as if he never will again. "For you, anything. I'll see you tomorrow, baby. Drive safe. I love you."

"I love you, too. See you tomorrow."

Gavin breaks our hug and starts toward his car, fingers still in mine until distance separates us. As he gets in his car, I get in mine. He and Micah talk a moment until he puts the car in gear.

I idle in the parking lot a moment, waving to Gavin as he and Micah drive off. He hasn't mentioned it, but tomorrow is Gavin's birthday and I want to surprise him. I want to host a game night. Ask everyone to bring food and drinks and laughter. Maybe decorate the house and have a cake. Make it one of his best birthdays yet.

Gavin and I may have been apart more than a decade, but some dates will be forever engraved in my heart. Including the day Gavin was brought into the world. And Gavin is definitely worth celebrating.

Eight years ago

TODAY IS the happiest and saddest day of my life.

November twenty-first.

Mine and Cora's anniversary. If we were still together, today would be our seventh anniversary. If it were a wedding anniversary, I would buy her something made of wool or copper. We would be corny like that, buying gifts according to outdated anniversary traditions. Finding unique ways to celebrate our time together.

But we haven't celebrated an anniversary together in over five years now. Not that I plan to celebrate this date as anything except ours. This day, until the day I die, will be ours.

Fuck.

I want to call her. Am desperate to hear her voice.

Would she still sound the same? Is she happy? Does she miss me like I fucking miss her? Some days, I don't have it in me to breathe, let alone exist in the world. Every time I talk with Micah, I ask vague questions about Shelly in the hopes he will give me a hint of something regarding Cora. But he gives nothing away. And it fucking sucks. He knows I won't come right out and ask, so he dances around my inadvertent questions.

Rather than hunt for a gift I will never give Cora, I opt for something else. Something permanent that will add a piece of her to me. A lifelong reminder—not as if I need one, but somehow this enhances our bond. With things booming in my career, I have gone back and forth for weeks about this. But it is my fucking body and I will do with it what I please.

I walk into the tattoo shop and walk up to the reception area. A young woman with fluorescent green hair peeks up from her magazine. She swivels the lollipop in her mouth from left to right a few times. "What can I do for you?" She pops the lollipop from her lips, licks them, then puts the lollipop back in her mouth. Don't know why, but it annoys the shit out of me.

"I have an appointment with Talon," I say.

She scans the screen before clicking the mouse. "I need a copy of your ID and for you to fill out this paper." She hands me a clipboard. While she makes a copy of my license, I read over, fill out, and sign the form. She hands me back my license. "He'll be with you in a minute. You can have a seat." She points to a leather couch off to the side and goes back to her magazine as if I never walked in.

"Thanks," I mumble.

A few minutes later, a burly man greets me and introduces himself as Talon. His arms are sleeved with a mishmash of tattoos. Muscles twice the size of mine. A bald head with full facial hair. And he towers over me by at least five inches, which is saying something considering I am six-two. Intimidating is definitely an adjective I would associate with this guy.

Talon leads me to a small cubicle with a black leather seat. He tugs a lever and flattens the table. "Have a seat, man. Here's the image you sent me." He slides a paper toward me. "This is what you want, right?"

"Yeah, between my shoulder blades," I reply.

Talon nods. "Is the size good? Or you want it bigger?"

I study the image a moment. Go big or go home, right? "Let's go a little bigger. Whatever you think will look best with the space."

He walks away and I stare around the booth. The short walls are littered with photos of other tattoos Talon has done. They range from intricate to minimal. Symbols and portraits and watercolor and quotes. Some with tons of color, others done with thin lines of black ink. Seeing all these photos—a portfolio of sorts—is reassurance this guy has done enough tattoos to not fuck mine up.

When he walks back into the booth, he shows me the new, larger version of the tattoo. "Look good?"

"Perfect. Thanks, man."

Talon directs me to take off my shirt, lay on the table, and find a comfortable position for my arms. He tells me how long he thinks the tattoo will take and that we will take occasional breaks, if needed. After everything is prepped and ready, he dips the tattoo gun in the ink and presses a peddle. When the buzz erupts next to me, I startle.

"You have any other tattoos, man?" Talon prompts.

"Nope. This is the first."

"Virgin skin," he says with a wicked gleam in his eye and wide grin on his lips. "My favorite."

The buzz cracks again and a sting pricks my skin. I close my eyes and take a deep breath. Sweat breaks out across my skin as adrenaline floods my veins. As he moves the needle over my skin, a blend of pain and thrill courses through me. Each line of ink he impregnates my skin with, I grow one step closer to Cora. She is the only reason I would mar my skin with something so permanent.

An hour into the tattoo, Talon asks me why I am getting a *Lord of the Rings* tattoo.

Not many people in California know Cora's and my history. I have mentioned things about her to Alyson and

Layla, but never her name and never too much detail. Cora is my heart. Something I have no intention on spreading like free samples. Even though we have been apart for years, I hug her essence close to my chest and protect it with every breath.

"My soul mate." It's all I say.

But that isn't enough for Talon. He wants more. "You're getting a tattoo for a girl? Shouldn't that be hearts or butterflies? Maybe initials or a date?"

He teases me, knowing I will tell him more. And he is right. "Nah, she's not a hearts and butterflies kind of girl. She is, on the other hand, addicted to *Lord of the Rings*. So, this is fitting and perfect."

Talon teases me further. "Aren't you a sweetheart. Does she have a tattoo for you?"

His question is innocent, but it gets under my skin and stabs at the throbbing organ beneath my sternum. "No, she hasn't gotten any ink yet." At least not that I am aware of. I haven't seen her in years, but I couldn't imagine her getting a tattoo without purpose. Talon doesn't need such information, though.

A few hours pass before the tattoo gun goes silent. He sprays something on a paper towel and swipes it over my newly tattooed skin. Although my skin is slightly numb, the wiping stings. A minute later, he helps me up and hands me a hand mirror. "Use that to check it out on the wall mirror." He points to a floor-length mirror opposite his booth.

I walk over and turn my back to the wall mirror and hold up the one in my hand. Twisting to see from different angles, I glance over the black ink on my back. Absolutely perfect.

"What's it say?" Talon asks as I stare at the mirror. "Elvish, right?"

"Yeah. Above the stars it says *love*. At the roots, it says *forever*. *Lord of the Rings* fan?"

"Only seen them once, but remembered the tree. So, I assumed the writing. Your girl will love it, man. The nipple piercings, too."

"Thanks."

One day, I hope she gets to see it.

Present

THE STEREO BLARES in the living room. Queen's "Another One Bites The Dust" at a volume way too loud for this early in the morning.

Micah comes up and taps my shoulder. "Get up, brother. Happy motherfucking birthday."

You have got to be fucking kidding me. I groan, roll to face the back of the couch, and smother myself with the pillow over my face. "Go away. It's too fucking early for this bullshit."

"Nope." He yanks the pillow from my hands. "I haven't celebrated a damn birthday with you in years. We're rectifying that right now. Up you go." He tugs the blanket off me and walks away, whistling like a cocky bastard.

"Asshole," I grumble as I sit up. "What time is it?"

Micah walks back into the room, pillow and blanket gone, and tosses a shirt at me. "Almost ten. For us normal folks, early was three hours ago. Uppity up." He steps up beside the couch and waves his hands as if to push me off.

"Since when do you get up early. Don't you mainly work at night? Like late?"

He doesn't respond.

After a minute, I get up and stumble to the bathroom. I crank the shower to scalding and step in. The water slowly washes the sleep off me, and soon I step out.

Once dressed, Micah suggests we go out for breakfast. I agree, but tell him he has to go with me to an appointment after. He directs us to a mom-and-pop restaurant where the line for a table is ten deep. After we get seated, we order breakfast and talk about everyone hanging out later tonight. He tells me he didn't hang around everyone else while I was in California because it felt weird. Supposedly, he has no idea what tonight entails, but I believe he knows more than he lets on.

Micah changes the topic and asks why Jonas pulled me aside last night. Says he checked on us from his spot in the arcade a few times. I smile and relay the conversation. Good to know Micah always has my back, even when I don't know it.

"That's pretty ballsy of him," Micah states. "No lie,

he's spent a lot of time with Cora. I'm shocked they've only remained friends all this time."

"Yeah, we touched on that when he admitted he was in love with her."

"And what did he say?"

I chuckle. "He said he's actually tried a couple of times to push for more, but she stopped him. The only time she didn't was when I left, and she was pissed and drunk. She leaned in to kiss him and he cut her off. Told her he didn't want to be a backup option. She told him how sad she was and that she just wanted to feel something again."

When Jonas told me that last tidbit, I cringed. I did that to her. Made her so desperate for affection she was willing to fall into the arms of someone she didn't love. Not romantically, anyway. Hearing the truth was a hundred punches to the gut. I never want her heart to feel such depravity again. Never want her to be desperate for love because she feels she has none.

"Dude, that's some crazy shit. All in all, he's a good guy. He's never done anything horrible to Cora, Shelly, or Erin. Their relationship is odd, but they all have a good time together. I hate to say it, but he helped her smile again."

"Fuck."

"Don't beat yourself up over it. For years, there was nothing you could do about it. And you can't change the past. It's done. So now, you just move forward. She loves you, bro. Always has, always will. He just kept her afloat while you were gone. Be thankful for that. Some of the shit Shelly told me painted a pretty ugly picture. She didn't leave her house for months after you left. Almost flunked school. A lot of people were worried about her."

Although Cora and I stopped talking after a couple months, she was always front and center in my mind. The times we did talk after I moved to California, she never portrayed what Micah tells me now. She masked her pain, and she did it well. Either that or I relieved it when we talked. I can only imagine how it all went to shit when I stopped talking with her altogether. Every time I hear a new snippet about our time apart, the fault line in my heart opens wider.

But I deserve the pain. Deserve to let it tear me apart inside. Every horrible memory. All the sleepless nights and days of depression. Because her pain is my pain. And I pledge to never let her experience such pain again.

Micah and I eat breakfast in silence. Once we finish, we pay and head to my appointment. I crank the radio while we drive, silencing any further conversation. I need to clear my head and music is my favorite form of therapy.

When we pull into the parking lot, Micah laughs loud enough I hear him over the music. After I cut the engine, Micah asks, "So what irreversible decision are you making today?"

"Shut the fuck up." I get out of the car and walk into the tattoo shop, Micah following in my wake.

I go through the normal spiel with the lady at the front counter, filling out the form and providing identification, then sit and wait to be called back. She twirls her pink hair and pops her bubblegum loudly.

Ten minutes later, I sit in a chair with my shirt off. The artist prints the tattoo and Micah is staring at me with a gleam in his eyes.

"Speak your mind," I tell him.

"You're really going to do this?" Micah asks.

"Isn't it rather obvious I'm doing this?"

"You can still back out."

"Backing out is not an option." I shake my head at him.

"But this is different than the other one, bro. And it doesn't get more permanent."

I cock my brow at him. "Actually, other permanent things have also crossed my mind."

Just as Micah is about to give me a ration of shit, the tattoo artist walks back in. He verifies I want the tattoo on my left pec and presses the layout to my skin. A couple minutes later, the tattoo gun is piercing my skin and a new form of euphoria filters through my bloodstream. This is different from the last tattoo. More. Everlasting. And I wouldn't change it for anything.

"So, who's Cora?" the artist asks.

"Girlfriend," I say. Micah makes a face that indicates

otherwise. "Although, I'm hoping she'll be more one day." At this, Micah shakes his head.

"Don't we all, man. My old lady and I have been together for years. Can't imagine life without her. Just haven't bucked up the courage to ask her yet. You?"

"Soon."

"Really?" Micah asks in disbelief. "You have got to be shitting me."

I drill holes in his head with my death stare. "Yeah. Why would you think otherwise? She's it for me, bro. Always has been. Just because you turned into a manwhore..."

"Let's not talk about me right now. We'll be here all day. Maybe we should be talking about the fact that you plan to marry Cora. Have you asked her?"

The artist laughs at our banter. "Not yet. But I'm not waiting. When the time comes, it's happening."

"You're ridiculous," Micah says.

"Why? Because I love her? Because I refuse to fuck this shit up again? Nothing will keep me from her now or in the future."

Before Micah chimes in with something snarky, the artist speaks up. "You two whine like a pair of bitches." He laughs, then goes back to the tattoo.

I tip my head back and close my eyes, shutting Micah out and dropping our conversation. He is such a pain in my ass sometimes. When the tattoo is done, I check it in a mirror and pay the artist.

When we get back in the car, Micah speaks up for the first time in an hour. "What's the French line?"

I tell him the line I memorized a lifetime ago. "Tu es les étoiles de ma lune. It translates to *you are the stars to my moon*."

"You really are lost," he says before laughing and cranking the music.

"In the best way. One more stop to make, okay?"

He nods. "Yeah, sure. Where to now?" I don't answer him as we pull onto the street and head south. He shakes his head and shrugs. "Whatever, bro. It's your day."

Damn right it is.

We arrive at Cora's house just before six. In her driveway is her Subaru, a motorcycle and a Beetle. I park behind her car and glance over to the window by the back patio. Through a crack in the curtains, I spot people running around like rapid fire. I squint and shift my head to the side to get a better view, but don't see anything else.

What the hell are they doing in there?

"Don't be upset," Micah says. When I shift to look at

him with narrowed eyes, he shrugs. "She wanted to do something for your birthday."

For the first time in years, my birthday isn't an upsetting day. In fact, this is the best birthday I have had since my teens. Heat spreads through me like warm honey. She intentionally planned a gathering for my birthday. Not just so she and I could spend time together, but also so others could celebrate too. God, I missed celebrating birthdays and holidays and monumental occasions with her. They were never elaborate, but she added flare to the day.

"I'm not upset," I say. "Far from it. Best birthday I've had in a while."

We step out of the car and take our time walking to the back door. No doubt Micah texted Shelly as we got closer, so it should be no surprise when we knock. Just as I bring my hand up to knock, the door flies open and Cora stands on the other side. She is all smiles and slightly out of breath.

My girl. *My. Girl.*

"I was beginning to wonder how long you were going to sit in the driveway," she says.

"You knew we were out here?" I ask.

"Yeah. Shelly saw you turn onto the street. Come in, come in." She waves us in and her excitement is infectious.

Micah steps past her and wanders into the house. But I step up to her, my mouth an inch from hers. "Thank you. This is perfect." I wrap my arms around her and kiss her forehead.

"You're welcome. Glad you like it."

"I love it. I love you."

She squeezes me tighter. "I love you, too. Come on, everyone is waiting."

We step into her small house. Once in the open space, I scan the rooms. Added to her normal decor are shiny happy birthday banners and cheesy kid's decor. On one wall is a plastic version of pin the tail on the donkey. The moment I see it, I burst out laughing. She loops her arm in mine and keeps us going forward.

On the kitchen countertop is a small round cake, *Happy Birthday* piped in white over the black icing. Next to the cake is an array of finger foods and alcohol. When I glance over at the dining table, which has a couple chairs added to the ends, I spot a small pile of gifts next to a stack of board and card games.

"I vote food first," I say.

"Second that," Micah chimes in.

And just like that, we all clamber into a line and grab platefuls of finger foods. We clear the games and gifts from the table and gather around to eat. When our plates are almost empty, Shelly pipes up and suggests I choose the first game. I riffle through the choices and go with the adult version of Watch Your Mouth.

For the next thirty minutes, each of us slobbers over semi-dirty phrases that sound absolutely filthy. Cora tries for a solid two minutes to say something no one can translate. While this happens, I pull out my phone and record a video of the whole show. I will definitely be watching that over and over. After we have all laughed our asses off, we opt to take a game break and dish out cake.

Cora and Shelly make a show out of adding twenty-nine candles to the cake and lighting them. The lights go out and everyone sings happy birthday to me as Cora holds the cake between us. The entire time everyone sings, I stare at her. Watch the mini-candle flames flicker on her skin. Take in her smile, remembering how long it has been since I saw her smile like this. Genuine and wide and happily. When the song finishes, I silently wish to spend every day of the rest of my life with Cora, then blow out all twenty-nine candles in one breath.

Cora smiles, then takes the cake in the kitchen. She hands me a big enough piece of cake for two and I take it back to the table while she finishes cutting it.

With a forkful of chocolate cake in my mouth, Shelly shoves the stack of gifts toward me. "Happy Birthday, Gavin."

I thank her after I swallow. "You didn't have to buy me anything." After I shove another bite in my mouth, I unwrap the small box. As soon as I see the package, I spit cake out of my mouth. "What the hell, Shelly?" Thank fuck Cora is still in the kitchen messing with cake. Not sure if she would be embarrassed or giggly or shocked.

I stare down at the one-hundred-count box of condoms and shake my head. When I peek up at Shelly, she shrugs in the same manner Micah does. "Not like you won't use them. Especially if you guys are back together. Plus, they were on sale at Costco."

As discreetly as possible, I wrap the paper around the box again and push it aside. The other two gifts are simple and normal. A gift card and a card with cash. Somehow, I will use the cash and card to buy them all something in return. I don't need gifts as long as I have Cora. She is the greatest gift of all.

For the next two hours, we play cards and shoot the shit with each other. Tonight is the most enjoyable evening and birthday I have had in a long time and I bask in the sentiment. My mom or parents always did nice things for me over the years, but it was never the same as when I was with Cora. Now that she is back in my life, I will never let anything break us apart again.

Erin yawns and it starts a ripple effect throughout the room. Within ten minutes, Erin, Shelly, and Micah pile into Shelly's car, and Jonas hops on his motorcycle. In the blink of an eye, only me and Cora stand in her house. And the solitude is heaven.

I help her clean up a few things that need to be put away now. After, we sit on the couch and simply hold each other. Only with her is silence comforting. I close my eyes and enjoy the warmth radiating off her and soothing me. Reminisce in the affection and warmth we once shared as I dream about what the future holds.

"Do you want to watch a movie?" she whispers into the dim-lit living room.

"Only if you want to. I'm content like this."

She turns into me more and presses her hand over my heart. I suck in a breath when her weight covers a portion of my new tattoo. Her eyes widen at my expression. "Are you okay? What's the matter?"

I sit up a little and kiss her forehead. "Yeah, baby. I'm okay. Just got a new tattoo today."

Cora perks up next to me. "You got a new tattoo? Can I see it?"

Eventually, I knew Cora would see my new tattoo. I just had no idea it would be tonight. Not that I fear her seeing it. Only curious how she will react.

I scoot forward a few inches and tug my shirt over my head, tossing it aside. The moment she sees it, all air leaves the room. "Gavin," she gasps. "I... I don't know what to say."

As I sit back against the cushion, she shifts closer to me. Her fascination with the ink is cute. By the way she studies it, I know she wants to run her fingers over it. "It'll heal over the next week," I inform her.

Her eyes well as she peeks up at me. "You know that's forever, right?"

"You are my forever, Cora. No other name will brand my skin. No other woman will have my heart. It has belonged to you since the first day of high school. The day I joined you under that tree and you drew me beside you on a sketch pad."

Tears spill from her eyes. "You're my forever, too. I tried to move on for so many years. Tried to care for another person. God, how I tried. But it never happened. Even when I tried to force it. Because I could never imagine life with someone other than you. So, I tucked you away for safekeeping in the hopes you would return."

I pinch the ends of her hair and play with it between my fingers. Fuck, I want to kiss her. But I promised I wouldn't kiss her until she initiated the kiss. And fuck if that isn't the most difficult vow to keep right now. Because everything about this day, this moment, cries out for me to lean forward and press my lips to hers.

She brings a hand to my other pec and skims over the flesh. Electricity shoots through every atom, cell, and molecule in my body. I swear to god, if she doesn't kiss me soon, I will break my promise. Because as patient as I am, this is pure torture.

Just as I am ready to cave on my desires, she leans forward and presses her lips to my left pec, an inch above the tattoo. "I love you," she says, breath hot on my skin.

And a switch flips inside me. Fire heats my blood, scorches my skin, has me panting for breath. I become a starved man and Cora is what my body needs to survive.

THE MOMENT I kiss Gavin's chest, a ticking time bomb detonates beneath my lips. As if my lips on his skin is the invitation he has been waiting for. The key to solve a riddle.

Before I grasp what is happening, Gavin scoops me up in his arms and walks toward my bedroom. A moment later, he tosses me on the bed and crawls over me. His lips brand my navel as he shoves my shirt up my torso and over my head. Every press of his lips is kindling added to a raging inferno inside me. An inferno that has always been there, but faded with his absence.

He peppers kisses across my collar bone and up my neck, nipping and sucking. His forearms press into the mattress on either side of me and cage me in. I knead the sides of his ribcage and around his backside, digging my nails into his bare flesh.

"Oh god, Gavin," I gasp, tipping my head back.

His lips graze my jawline and finally land on my mouth. Liquid heat swipes across my lower lip and begs me to open up for him. The second his tongue brushes against mine, I lose all coherent thought. Gavin is everywhere. The saltiness of his lips on my skin mingles with my taste buds. His fevered skin heats up every inch of my skin. The piney-beach scent only Gavin has seeps into my senses. Fuck, it's too much.

He hovers above me a second. "I want you, baby. To be inside you."

"God, yes."

As soon as I grant him permission, Gavin's hands travel to my waist and unfasten my jeans. He jostles them down my hips and yanks them to my ankles before depositing them on the floor. The pads of his fingers graze the tips of my toes and slowly descend over the tops of my feet. "Do you know how long I've waited for this?" Heat dances over my ankles and ascends my shin. "How long I've waited to see you?" Tingles play over my knee and tease the distal end of my thigh. "To touch you." Sparks ignite in my quads and I squirm beneath him. "To love you."

His hands reach my hips and I am ready to explode from anticipation. But he remains idle, his fingers toying with the bands of my panties. I pant and wriggle beneath him. "So, what are you waiting for now?" I tease, egging him on.

A smirk tugs at the side of his mouth. "Baby, I'm just reveling in the moment. I won't take you or us or our lives for granted. Never again."

"Gavin…" I whisper into the darkness.

He lowers himself and presses a sweet, earnest kiss to my lips. Packed with intensity and longing and hope. "I love you, Cora. I have loved you for as long as I can remember. And I will love you for the rest of my days." We kiss as if the past thirteen years never happened, as if time was never stolen from us, and the world rights itself again. Stars burn brighter. Planets align. And everything goes back in its rightful place.

As our lungs gasp for air, Gavin breaks the kiss and his lips trace my ear and down my neck. He massages the sides of my torso as he lavishes kisses down my sternum, between my breasts, and stops at my navel. Fingers skirt around my backside and unhook my bra. Heated breaths paint my navel for three unshakable beats before his hands glide out and slip the black barrier from my breasts.

Neither of us moves for a moment. Instead, we lay impossibly still and absorb everything about this experience. The last time Gavin saw this much of my body, I was a sixteen-year-old girl. Although my body hasn't changed drastically over the last thirteen years, I am not the same. And neither is he. Not just our bodies, but also who we are as people. Yes, I am still that girl under the tree in the courtyard who fell desperately in love with

Gavin Hunt. A boy who only wanted to share the shady tree with me.

But now, I am the woman who has fallen in love all over again. The woman who is brave enough to give myself over to him, wholeheartedly. As heartbroken and devastated as I was over the last thirteen years, I forgive him for the things he could not control. Things neither of us could control. For all the moments he wanted to come back to me and was unable to. As much as I tried to deny it, Gavin was always here. Tucked away in my heart. Rooted deep in my bones. Flowing through my veins. Hiding in the corners of my mind. Holding me captive. Telling me to be patient and wait for him. I see this now. All these reasons are why I was never able to truly let anyone else into my heart. Because Gavin had it. *Has* it.

And he always will.

"I love you, Gavin," I whisper as I comb my fingers through his hair.

He shudders above me before he feathers a kiss to my navel. The pads of his fingers imprint my back, my sides, my hips. They knead and paw and bruise in the most delicious way. His kisses transition from sweet to hungry and ravenous. I curl my fingers into fists and tug his hair as my back arches off the bed and I gasp at his touch. Gavin nips along the hemline of my underwear until he reaches my hip. He sucks and sucks and sucks, and it is not until a moment later that I realize he is marking me.

Claiming me. As his. The notion of his lips and tongue bruising my skin sets me on fire and I moan.

After he is satisfied with his work, he raises enough to peer up at me. "Fuck. The way your soul coos for me, baby. You're my own personal heaven and I never want to leave."

"Never."

"Never," he repeats.

Gavin slips his fingers beneath the band of my panties, grazes the skin below one, two, three times, then hooks the cotton in his grip and peels it away from my body. After he tosses them to the floor, he stands at the foot of the bed and ogles every inch of me. His steely eyes sear my flesh as he takes in every inch of me.

Normally, I would be shy under such scrutiny. But with Gavin, I crave his appraisal. Long for his eyes to drink in every fragment of my wanton body. Beg for his undeniable *need* for me.

Over the years, I never allowed this with the few people I'd been with. Never let them that close to me. Hell, I never removed my clothes. I was good with celibacy.

But with Gavin... I willingly bared every aspect of myself to him. Heart. Soul. The good, bad and ugly. He is the missing piece. My forever. The be-all and end-all. And there will never be anything that stands between us.

My eyes lock on his for three panting breaths before he breaks the connection. His drift down the lines and curves of my body, and mine do the same. Down his neck, across his collar bones, the hollow spot at the base of his throat. When I get to his pecs, I groan as I read my name permanently imprinted on his skin. Who knew something so simple could be the hottest display of affection. My heart is a fierce monster beneath my breast bone —pound, pound, pounding to be set free.

In my periphery, Gavin unbuttons and lowers his shorts. Black boxer briefs barely contain his erection, and I unabashedly stare at his groin. *Was he always that big?* I swallow and know he hears it.

He palms his erection through the cotton. "See something you like, baby?" A hint of sarcasm laces his question.

"You have no idea," I say, brazen.

My eyes pop back to his as he shoves his underwear to the floor. A second later, he presses a knee into the mattress and crawls back up my body. No barriers. No secrets. Just me and Gavin.

He kisses up my stomach, my breast, my neck, and stops when we are eye to eye. "I want nothing between us, Cora. Ever." He inhales deeply and shuts his eyes a second. "I've always used condoms. It's been a while since the last… and I got tested after."

I reach up and lace my fingers behind his neck, draw him down to me and press my lips to his. He doesn't want either of us to admit that we have been with other people since each other. Doesn't want to tell me the ways he filled the void. And neither do I. But this is us. Open. No holds barred. No skeletons.

"Thank you." I kiss him again. "I've been tested, too. And I'm on the pill."

His whole body relaxes. A second later, his lips are on mine as he grinds his length against the apex of my thighs. I lift my hips and add more pressure. And god is it amazing. His pecs squash my breasts as his abdomen slides against my belly. Strong hands frame my face and Gavin worships my mouth with his. I caress his biceps, the sides of his torso and slip my hands around to his lower back. Time has made Gavin's body a work of art. A sculpture. A god-like effigy worthy of worship and devotion.

I grab hold of his ass and paw at the muscular flesh in my palms. His hips rock into mine as his erection coasts up and down my entrance. A moment later, his palm grazes down my side and slips between us. With a lift of his hips, he slips his hand between my thighs and runs a finger over my slit.

"Fuck, baby," he growls. "You are so damn wet."

As his finger toys with my lower lips, I pivot my hips at the perfect time and his digit sinks inside me. It may be only one finger, but it consumes me. A second later, I rock forward again. Back and forth. Faster, faster. Gavin inserts another finger and I moan. His hand pistons as my hips plunge and we form the perfect rhythm.

As I fuck his fingers, he reveres my mouth, my neck,

my breasts. He is everywhere. Every molecule. Every fiber. Every beat of my heart and breath in my lungs. Too much and not enough at the same time. Breath and heat and sweat. Friction and passion. While one hand pistons inside me, his other slides into my hair and clutches at the crown. He locks me in place with his grip and his lips and his fingers.

Fire blazes hot in my epicenter. Building faster, hotter. Gavin nips along my jaw and stops at my ear. "So fucking hot, baby," he whisper-growls. Then sucks at the spot just behind my ear. The one only he knows about. The spot that tips me over the edge.

White hot heat detonates low in my belly and ricochets through every muscle. I pinch my eyes shut and stars glow on the backs of my lids. I bow into his body as mine clutches his fingers with every ounce of strength. High pitch gasps for air whine from my lungs and Gavin crashes his mouth to mine. Dizziness warps my vision as I ride the wave of my high.

For a moment, we lay motionless—Gavin hovering above me. Panting as the scent of sex floats in the air. I haven't had an orgasm like that in years. Too many years. And I want more. So much more.

"Gavin?"

"Yeah, baby?" His breaths as labored as my own.

I kiss along his jaw and graze the flesh with my teeth before reaching his lips. Pressing one, two, three kisses to the soft lips I could lose myself in for days on end. When

I break the kiss, I frame his face with my hands and lock eyes with him. Then kiss him one last time. "Please, I need you inside me," I whimper.

A growl reverberates low in his diaphragm and ripples into me like a tidal wave. He scoops one arm around the back of my shoulders and the other around my hips. Before I realize what is happening, he flips us over and straddles me over his thighs. All the times we had been together years ago, I never sat atop him. Never had control when we had sex. And now, I feel like a goddess. Like the master of our world. Of Gavin.

"Ride me, baby," he purrs.

His request is gasoline to the fire blazing in my belly, I press my palms flat on his chest, lift myself and position my entrance over his cock. Inhaling deeply, I lower myself onto him slowly. Inch by inch, I take him to the hilt and audibly gasp once I am seated.

Gavin sets his hands on my hips and locks me in place. And for a moment, neither of us moves. We relish in being connected like this once again. Skin to skin. Completely vulnerable. Absolute exposure.

His breathing spikes and I lean down and take his mouth with mine. The kiss starts slow. Sweet, gentle pecks. Then I paint his lower lip with my tongue and he invites me in. Our tongues taste and devour one another for a beat. And then I rock my hips back and slam them forward.

He breaks our kiss, my mouth an inch above his, and

hisses. "Fuuuuck…"

I do it again, sinking my nails into the flesh just beneath his pecs. When I roll my hips again, Gavin thrusts up and hits a spot deep inside me, a place only he reaches, and I cry out. One thrust, then another, until we find a rhythmic dance only two lovers know. His hands roam my abdomen and my breasts before he sits up. One, two, three more rocks of my hips and I orgasm a second time.

A second passes and before I catch my breath, Gavin flips us back over and hovers above me. "Wrap your legs around me, baby."

I do as he says, locking my ankles together, and he thrusts hard and fast into me. Gone are the moments of sweet caresses and gentle strokes. Now, the inferno blazing between us is set to atomic levels. And if this burn doesn't get satiated, both of us will implode.

Gavin buries his face in the crook of my neck, lips and tongue sucking my skin. One arm braces my shoulder while the other clutches my hip. He pumps in and out of me—faster, harder, hungrier. His mouth, his cock, his heart, it is almost too much to bear. Almost.

Sweat pulses from our pores and slicks us from head to toe. His breath hot on my neck as his teeth clamp down on the tender skin. Our cries of pleasure mingle in the air and bounce off the walls. And I climb, climb, climb back up the peak once again. "Oh god, Gavin. Don't. Fucking. Stop," I pant out.

His grip on me tightens as his hips buck harder. He grunts into my skin, and I know he resists his own need to come. Resisting so we can prolong this reunion. And that fact sets me off again. Has my walls constricting and my vision fading.

My body a limp noodle as I come down from my orgasm. Gavin brings his lips back to mine, kisses them tenderly, and whispers, "One more, baby." I nod and he pulls out of me, flips me on my belly, and hikes my ass in the air.

With my profile against the sheets, I stretch my arms above my head and clutch the pillows in my fists. He lines himself up with my entrance, but doesn't push inside. Not yet. He leans over me and whispers in my ear. "I love you to the ends of the earth, Cora. Forever." When he lifts off of me, his fingertips dance over my neck before tracing down the length of my spine to the base of my tailbone. It is more than just a touch. It is devotion. Awe. Adulation. Reverence. Intimacy. Worship.

With both hands squeezing my hips, he eases inside of me. Each inch forward is a step closer to heaven. Closer to where Gavin and I will be for all eternity. Together. Connected. Unbreakable. Inseparable.

When he is fully seated inside me, I mewl into the sheets and tighten my fists. He relaxes his hands for a split second before clamping down harder. Tomorrow, my body will artfully display the evidence of our reunion. And I plan to revel in every single line and stroke and strawberry on my skin. Cherish them and create new ones before they fade. Memorize the feel of them and how they came to be.

Gavin doesn't move for a minute and I peer over my shoulder at him. His eyes closed and brow furrowed. Before I open my mouth to ask if everything is okay, a tear rolls down his cheek. I push up so I'm on my hands and knees, ready to spin around and soothe whatever sadness has taken hold. Just as I straighten, he presses a palm flat between my shoulder blades and presses me down to the bed.

"Gavin, are you okay?" I ask, genuinely worried.

His hand rests between my scapulae a beat before gliding back to my hip. "Never better, baby," he chokes out.

"Then why are you crying?"

My eyes still trained on his as he stares down at me. "Because I haven't been this happy in a really long time."

"Happy tears?" I ask because I have to be certain.

"Yes, baby. Happy tears." And then he rocks his hips back and drives forward.

He fills me so fully, I forget how to breathe. How to speak. My eyes roll back and I groan. "Oh fuck…"

In. Out. Stroke after stroke, he brings us both closer to nirvana. His hips slap my ass, balls whack my clit, head of his cock rubs the nerve endings inside my walls. Building. Climbing. Taller. Higher. His tempo increases and I know he is trying to get me there before he lets go.

As if confirmation of my thoughts, his hand snakes around my waist and his finger circles my clit. His hips piston faster as our moans consume every lick of empty space in the room.

"Gavin..." I wring the sheets in my fists. "So close. Don't stop."

He adds more pressure to my clit and circles faster as his hips thrust like a well-oiled machine. I clamp my eyes shut as my breath comes in short, staggered whimpers. On the next stroke, the head of his cock strokes perfectly over the nerve cluster in my walls and I detonate. A grunting scream rips from my throat as he continues to slam into me. My vision blanks as I convulse and milk his cock.

My orgasm feels like a never-ending stream of consciousness as Gavin releases inside me. Only when his hips slow and he collapses over top of me, does my body calm down.

"Holy shit," he breathes into my hair.

Gavin rests his head beside mine, arms clutching my breasts and belly, and heaves. No intimacy compares to what Gavin and I share. It isn't just the sex—although sex with Gavin is literal euphoria.

Intimacy with Gavin is so much more. Friendship and love. Sunsets and strolls in the park. Shared whispers and tender kisses. Side glances and subtle smiles. Speaking without words. Acceptance. An incomparable bond. A life force all its own. The promise of forever.

My hips drop to the mattress and I relax more than I have in thirteen years. Gavin lays beside me and I roll to face him. He drags me closer to him, weaves our legs together, and plays with the ends of my hair. Tenderness bleeds from his pores into mine. So pure and true. He leans in and kisses my lips, the tip of my nose, then my forehead.

When our breathing regulates, he traces my cheekbones with his finger, then my lips—his eyes fixed on the movement. One, two, three heartbeats later, his gray eyes lock on mine. Gets lost in them. We lay like this for minutes or hours, entranced with each other. No words are spoken—not that they need to be. We simply breathe each other in. Realign our souls. Remember the feeling of us.

For the next several hours, we memorize every inch of the other's body. Learn all the new lines and curves and dips and scars. And get lost in paradise time and time again.

I peek over Gavin's shoulder at the clock and check the time. Five twenty-one. For the last seven-plus hours, we have worshiped one another. And although I would love nothing more than to pass out wrapped in his arms right now, a different idea pops in my head.

I bolt up and fumble through the darkness. "Cora, what are you doing?" His mumble is sweet and inquisitive as he props himself up on his elbows.

"Get dressed. I want to go somewhere."

Gavin glances at the clock, then flops on his back. "Come back to the bed and cuddle with me. We can go later." As adorable as he is in this very moment, I resist the temptation of falling back into the sheets with him.

After stepping into a fresh pair of lacy boy short panties, I slip on a pair of black jeans. "Can't wait. It's time sensitive."

Gavin sits up and stares at me as I yank a shirt from a hanger. In the dark, I have no idea what shirt it is, nor do I care. I tug it over my head then walk over to the bed and grab his hand. He gives in and stands up, pulling me to his chest and kissing me. "Okay, baby. Where are we going?" he asks as he locates his clothes and dresses.

"It's a surprise. But you'll love it. Promise."

While Gavin finishes dressing, I head out to the kitchen, feed and love on Luna, and make us both a large to-go mug of coffee. When he emerges from the bedroom, I hand him a steaming mug and place a kiss on his cheek. We're quiet as we walk out the back door and get into my car. After a little maneuvering around Gavin's car, we get on the road as I speed toward our destination.

Less than thirty minutes later, we land on Central Avenue in downtown St. Petersburg and head toward the water. The streets are still dark, but slowly waking up in the early morning hours. Soon, I park the car, feed a meter on Beach Drive and grab a blanket from the back of the car—one I kept back there to protect my camera equipment when I cart it onto the beach during shoots.

Gavin slips his hand around mine and I guide us near the waterfront. Near the new pier is a small man-made beach. We open up the blanket and spread it out on the sand. Gavin sits with knees up and legs spread, and I sit down between them. He wraps his arms around me and pins me close to his body.

"This is perfect, baby," he whispers, his chin resting on my shoulder as we stare out at the Bay.

I relax into him more. "It's time for a sunrise. Our lives have been filled with countless sunsets. Time to start fresh with new traditions. I want just as many sunrises as sunsets."

Sunrises are the start of something new and invigo-rating. Although Gavin and I have known each other for what feels like a lifetime, we hit a snafu. A fault we couldn't scale until the time was right. During that time, we grew. Into ourselves and into adulthood. We had the chance to discover who we are without each other. And fate still found a way to reconnect us. Make us whole again. Give us a chance to start anew.

A sunrise after the darkest sunset.

The sky pinks near the horizon and Gavin squeezes me tighter. "I'm sorry it took me so long to get back to you. Believe me when I say, if I had known it'd be this long, I would have done things differently."

I shake my head. "No, Gavin. Everything is how it's meant to be. Was our time apart the most gut-wrenching experience of my life? Yes. There has been no pain worse than losing you. Never will be. But would I change any of it? I don't think I would. It sounds wrong, but I think the years have taught us so much. Taught us how to love. Showed us what we'd miss without one another. Many couples stay together for years and grow unhappy with their relationship. A rift divides them and they fall out of love." I pause, take a deep breath, and collect myself. "If that would've happened between us... as hurt as I was when we lost touch, I never stopped loving you. I suppressed it. Smothered it. Buried it deep in the corners of my heart and packed it tight with dirt. But it has always been there."

Gavin inhales deeply and drags me impossibly closer to him. "I could never not love you, Cora Davies." Everything about his statement is permanent, carved in stone, and I fall inconceivably harder for him.

The light pink sky blooms into a hot pink-orange as the sun edges closer to the horizon. Darkness fades from the sky as a faint blue comes into view. Another couple walks onto the sand and sits fifty feet from us, phone out and snapping images of the glowing scenery.

I lean my head against Gavin and marvel in his warmth behind me. His arms holding me close. His fingers drawing soft patterns on my forearms. I sigh and feel the pain of the last thirteen years lift away. Beautiful colors paint the sky. A few clouds linger and add touches of lavender and gray. Feeling like I can finally breathe for the first time in over a decade, I whisper, "Life is perfect."

Gavin shakes his head beside me, and I turn to glimpse his expression. A smile stretches his face from ear to ear and displays his perfect white teeth. "There's only one thing that could make life perfect."

His steely-gray irises swirl with love and passion and admiration. I get lost in his eyes. Eyes I missed every day. Eyes no camera captured the way my memories did. Momentarily, I forget what he said and shake my head to snap myself out of the temporary fog.

"And what's that?" I ask, matching his smile.

He lifts an arm from my waist, cups my cheek, and brushes his thumb in small circles. I lean into his touch and sigh. His other arm holds me unimaginably closer. Eyes hold mine as he breathes slow and steady. Quiet for a beat, his expression turns intense. Fierce. One-hundred-percent serious. His lips part and I drop my gaze just as he licks them. "If you were my wife."

All air gets sucked from my lungs.

Three years ago

W OMEN SWARM THE ROOM, buzzing around like worker bees eager to aid the queen. The queen—actually, the bride—sits on a tall chair, labeled "Bride" in silver letters on the back, and breathes heavily while another woman does her makeup. Her thick, black locks are pinned back partially and curled. Eyelids brushed a soft blush. Lips coated in a neutral gloss. A subtle shimmer added to her skin.

Most brides are so nervous on their wedding day and never remember all the little moments. Like this one in the dressing room of the church. Which is why I am here. To capture the bride with her bridesmaids tending to her. Her mother keeping the bridesmaids—as well as people not in the room—in check. Novelty items such as jewelry and robes and hangers.

I bring the camera to my eye and snap a handful of images. Before anyone stepped foot in here, I walked around the grounds and took several photos of the church, flowers and various displays. The wedding is nowhere near luxurious. Sherrie—the bride—was adamant about keeping the ceremony clean and simple and pristine. Not an overabundance of flowers or decor. Whites and creams and a hint of blush-pink. Very subtle, but utterly breathtaking. The photos of her gown on the hanger will be coveted for years to come.

"Twenty minutes, ladies," a woman shouts from the door before disappearing.

As if that is the cue they have all been waiting for, everyone's pace triples. Bridesmaids zip each other up in their blush-colored gowns before removing the bride's dress from the hanger. Once the makeup artist steps away, the bridesmaids step front and center. I bring the camera back to my eye and snap continuously as they help her into her dress.

When the dress is in place, her maid of honor hands her the bouquet and everyone steps back a moment, allowing me to take some individual photos of her before she leaves the room. After I finish, hair and makeup step back up and double-check to make certain everything is perfect.

She makes such a beautiful bride. Something I will never be.

I shake off the errant thoughts and leave the bridal suite. A moment later, I knock on the door for the groom's suite. A guy with dark hair, gauge-pierced ears, and a wicked smile answers the door. For a moment, I flashback to another guy who had similar features, a guy I once cared about, but push it aside and slip on my professional mask.

I lift my camera and waggle it. "Is everyone decent? I'd like to get some photos of the groom's suite before the ceremony begins."

He peeks over his shoulder then steps aside and gestures me to enter. "Sure, we're dressed. Can't speak for decent," he snickers.

I ignore his insinuation and walk into the room. Snapping a few pictures, I tell the guys to do whatever it is they were doing before I came in. The guys relax and start joking with each other, slapping backs and teasing the groom about how he will only have one piece of ass for the rest of his life. But the groom lights up at the idea and I capture every little tweak in his lips. Every crinkled uptick near his eyes. Every ounce of joy he exudes.

Love is a funny thing. When you see it with your own eyes, it is unbelievable. Unparalleled. Simple touches— the way he tucks your hair behind your ear or toys with the ends of the strands or draws art on your skin with his fingers or holds you close every chance possible. A small upturn of the lips—just enough to let you know he is thinking of you. A slight lean of the body—because he can never be too close or get enough of you. Love sneaks up on you, slithers itself around your heart like vines, blankets you in warmth and security and joy, and blossoms like a field of wildflowers. It is incredible and incomparable and incomprehensible.

And I hope to never feel it again.

I take a few more photos of the groom and groomsmen, excuse myself, and head for the main area of the church. Once there, I walk in and photograph the crowd in the pews. Candid images of family and friends, old and young. People carry on conversations about how the bride and groom met and fell in love instantaneously. They recant how inseparable they are and how they never imagine them apart. After several more clicks of the shutter, I head back to where the bridal party will enter. And thankfully, away from all the puppy-love conversations.

It isn't as if I don't believe in love. Love is real and magical and undeniable. But love is also a rusty, jagged hunting knife in my chest. Twisting and depressing.

The music shifts and I take a deep breath. Ten seconds later, the groomsmen walk through the large wooden doors. I snap photo after photo. The guy who answered the door to the groom's suite passes me and winks. I continue taking photos and don't acknowledge the gesture. If I were any other woman, I would melt into a puddle at his feet. Swoon at the prospect of him asking me to dance later or grab a drink or exchange phone numbers. He is definitely gorgeous, but unfortunately for me, I am far from interested. In anyone. Ever.

I purse my lips, bring the camera to my eye, and continue photographing the wedding. After all the groomsmen pass, the music changes again. The wedding march—a standard, but elegant choice. Once upon a time, this song popped into my head. Impregnated visions of white gowns and black suits and promises of forever. But I was young and naïve then. I am neither of those things anymore. And after my dreams were obliterated, I am quite content becoming an old cat lady. At least as a cat lady, I will receive nothing but unconditional love.

The wedding passes and a million photos are taken. But it is not until the reception when I lose my shit.

Upbeat music fades from the sound system and the deejay speaks up. "This is for all the lovebirds in the room. Grab your guy or lady and head out to the dance floor."

A new song crackles through the speakers. A song I haven't heard in years. One that cracks my heart and cripples me on the spot. The twangy guitar intro to "Better Together" by Jack Johnson floods every available space in the room and drowns me instantly. Tears prick my eyes and, within seconds, roll down my cheeks. An emotional ball the size of a softball lodges in my throat.

I can't breathe.

Fuck. I can't be here. I can't be here.

The groomsman hottie approaches me, a smile plastered on his face until he notices my state. "Hey, you okay?"

I shake my head. It is too much. All of it. The bride, the groom, the promises, the happiness, the music. One big ball of happily ever after. Something I thought I would have. Until my heart got ripped from my chest and annihilated.

"I need to leave," I tell him. "Now."

"Do you need a ride? I can drive you."

As great as the idea sounds, I decline his offer. The last thing I need is to lose my shit with a guy that resembles the reason *why* I am crying. All that would lead to is another hot mess.

After I pack up my camera equipment, I find the bride and groom and apologize for my early departure. Thankfully, all the necessary photos for the wedding have been captured. Now it is just flat out party time. They hug and thank me and then I bolt out the door. Away from the reminder of broken promises.

When I reach my car, I set everything in the back then get in the car and lock the doors. I sit there, alone in the lot, for over thirty minutes, crying in my hands. Sobbing as if I am sixteen all over again.

Over the last decade, I have lost so much in my life. All of that loss wraps around one person.

Gavin Hunt.

Losing Gavin was like cutting out my heart with a spoon and tossing it in the darkest, deepest parts of the ocean. Without him, I had no reason to love. No desire to love. Nothing has changed. Over the years, brick by brick, I slowly built a towering wall around the space where my heart once sat. Reinforced it with steel beams and barbed wire. Hardened myself to everyone. Family. Friends. I would never allow someone to do to me what Gavin Hunt did—crush my heart and run away with my soul.

Right here, in the parking lot of the reception hall, where two lovers celebrate their joyous union, I make a vow to myself. A vow that will never be broken, because I hold the key. I am the gatekeeper of this truth.

"I will never open my heart to anyone ever again. I will never love another person ever again. And I most definitely will never marry anyone."

Present

"LIFE IS PERFECT," Cora whispers as we stare toward the rising sun.

Now that things are finally back as they should be, now that the stars have realigned and I can breathe, life is pretty great. But I wouldn't say life is perfect. Pretty close, but not quite.

I shake my head and Cora peers over at me. My smile stretches so tight my cheeks hurt. I can't help it. This is what she does to me—shines a light on every shadow, lifts me up, makes me feel alive and whole and worthy. When I am with her, life is worth living. A life with her is worth living.

"There's only one thing that could make life perfect," I tell her. For some reason, I feel as if I should be nervous.

Should have sweaty palms or be biting my lip or fidget-ing. But I don't have a nervous bone in my body. If anything, I have never felt calmer a day in my life.

Cora studies me intently, her vibrant green eyes glowing in sunrise. She scans my eyes and forehead before dropping to my lips. She is absolutely stunning right now and I make a mental note to see a million more sunrises with her at my side.

As if coming out of a daze, Cora shakes her head and asks, "And what's that?" A hint of teasing lingers on her tongue.

But I am dead serious. More serious than ever. More than any other time in my life. Nothing in my life or this world matters if Cora isn't beside me. And I want her beside me through it all. The good days and bad. Our young days and old. With children and grandchildren. I want it all, and only with her.

I peel one arm away from her waist, frame her cheek in my palm, and swipe my thumb over the soft skin below her cheekbone. As soon as I do, she leans her face into my palm and I scoot closer to her. I stare into her magnificent green irises—a perfect blend of the trees and the sea.

Cora is everything I want in my life. Beauty and charisma and spunk and passion. She holds the key to my heart and is the guardian of my soul. In the last thir-teen years, she has never left me—in spirit, anyway. Every woman I looked at was compared to her. And there was no contest. Hands down, Cora is it for me. There is not a single person walking this earth I want more than her. She gives me breath and life and purpose and love. Without her, I wander the earth with no destination.

"If you were my wife," I announce.

Cora gasps and freezes in my arms. For three of my breaths, she doesn't breathe once. And then she inhales deeply. Deeper than I have ever heard another person breathe. "Gavin…" She says my name as if it is her dying breath.

"Cora, I have spent far too much time away from you. Without you, I am a shell of a man. Every second we were apart, I merely existed. It wasn't until I saw you again that I remembered how to breathe. That my heart remembered it had another purpose other than beating. I dreamt of this day, but feared it would never happen. No more. Life is too short to not spend it with the person who matters most." I spin around to face her and prop myself up on one knee. "Cora, I know what life is like without you in it. I never wish to experience pain or darkness like that again. Nor do I want you to. The day my plane touched down here, I somehow knew life would be better. I didn't have the answers, but I felt it in my bones. And I wasn't wrong. How could it not be kismet bringing us back together? I belong to you, Cora. And I would be honored to be your husband. Will you marry me?"

Behind Cora, the other couple on the beach have their camera turned toward us. No doubt they're recording this. Another win in my favor.

Please let her say yes.

When she doesn't say anything for a moment, I remember the box is still in my pocket. Maybe if she sees the ring I bought, she will realize just how serious I am. I fish the soft, black box from my pocket and lift the lid. Nestled inside the box is a two-carat, square-cut black diamond in a tall setting. Along each edge of the black diamond are three smaller white diamonds. Several white diamond chips burrow in the titanium band from top to bottom. Hugging the engagement band is a matching wedding band with larger white diamonds.

Her hands fly to cover her mouth as she gasps. A second later, she lowers them to her chin. "Gavin…" she whispers. "Oh my god." Her glazed green eyes dart to mine and tears spill out, sliding down to her illustrious smile. "Yes. A million times yes." Cora crawls up on her hands and knees and launches herself at me. We fall to the sand and laugh.

I wrap my arms around her body and squeeze her with every ounce of strength I possess. "Fuck, baby. I love you so goddamn much."

After a minute, I sit us up and kiss the hell out of her. She tastes like salt and passion and forever. The best fucking taste in the world. And I am the luckiest man alive because she just said I get to keep her forever.

When the kiss breaks, I scoot back an inch and take the ring out of the box. She juts her left hand toward me and I slip the link to forever on her ring finger. The second it rests in place; the sun brightens the world more. I slam my mouth back on hers and kiss her as if she has already slipped a ring on my finger. The sooner, the better.

Forever will never be long enough with Cora. No matter how many lives we live, we will always find each other. Eternally.

After we dial down our public display, the couple from down the beach walks over and congratulates us. They offer to send us the video they recorded plus a few still pictures and I instantly jump on their offer, thanking them. We talk with them a few minutes before we shake out the blanket, fold it, and walk back to the car.

The second we get in the car, Cora's stomach grumbles and we decide to grab breakfast. As we head back toward Clearwater, I stare at the engagement ring on her finger. She isn't left-handed, but now she proudly drives with her left hand on the wheel. Every time the sun catches her ring just right, a halo flashes on the interior roof of the car.

Like an angel. My angel. My future wife.

After all these years, I wasn't sure if we would find our way back to each other. But we did. And I wasn't sure if I would see this day. This exact day. The day when

Cora and I were back together and she wore my ring on her finger.

And now that the day is here, an odd flutter ripples beneath my ribcage. The sensation light and exhilarating and eternal. Does she feel this fluttering right now? The exultation of finally living the life you were destined to live.

We pull into a parking lot and hop out of the car. Although we are both dog tired, there is enough adrenaline coursing through our veins to keep us both up all day. I sidle up to her left and slip my hand in hers, loving the way it feels when the ring grazes my palm. Until it comes to fruition, I imagine no other moment or emotion or experience topping this.

After we eat breakfast, Cora starts driving us back toward her house. As much as I want to lay in bed with her curled in my arms, there is something else I want to do. "Do you mind if we make another stop?" I ask.

She glances over at me a second, then faces the increasing traffic. The wind whips her hair across her profile as I inhale a hint of her frankincense-gardenia scent. "Yeah, sure. Where to?"

"I'll give you directions," I tell her.

I guide her through traffic for four or five miles before telling her to pull into a parking lot. When we park, she peers up at the sign, shakes her head, and laughs. "Really? Again?"

Laughing right alongside her, I shrug. "What can I

say? There's just something I need to do before we go home."

Cora cocks a brow at me and I know it is due to my casual reference to *home*. But she won't argue with me. For us, home has never consisted of four walls, a floor and a roof. Home has always been when we are together. "Alright."

We get out of the car and walk up to the storefront. I open the door and Cora's eyes scan every inch of the tattoo shop. Luckily, this shop is open more hours than most due to the number of artists. I walk up to the counter and the woman that looks up at me shakes her head. She is the same woman from yesterday. Hot pink hair, the front half rolled up and pinned close to her scalp, the back half left loose to her shoulders. She blows a bubble from her gum and lets it pop like it's second nature.

"Everything okay?" she asks. No hello or how are you. She must assume something is wrong with the tattoo I got yesterday.

"Everything is fantastic," I say and she rolls her eyes. "I'd like to get another tat."

"Oh," she perks up. "Well, the same artist who worked on you yesterday isn't here right now. You cool with that?"

"That's fine. It's nothing extravagant."

After a few minutes, I fill out the same form again and give her my ID. Once the formalities are out of the way, a woman comes out of the back. Her right arm is decked out in a full sleeve of ink. From what I can tell, it appears to reach her back as well. Her hair is a rich, dark brown and she has it pinned in a messy bun with a folded bandana tied at the top. She has this whole 1950s pinup girl/rockabilly vibe going on.

"Hi, I'm Autumn," she introduces herself and shakes my hand. "Looking for something specific today?"

"Gavin. Nice to meet you. Yeah, I want to get a wedding band tattooed on my ring finger."

Beside me, Cora sucks in a sharp breath. No doubt she wasn't expecting that. "Gavin, you don't need to do that," she says.

"I know, baby," I tell her. "But I want the world to know I belong to you. And no one else. Always."

Cora nods and doesn't utter a sound. The tattoo artist, Autumn, guides us back to her booth and has me sit in the chair. Currently, Cora and I are the only patrons in the building. Not having people coming and going right now is nice and odd at the same time. When the gun sparks, Cora startles next to me. I reach out and she takes my hand.

Twenty minutes later, I stare down at the thick black band at the proximal end of my fourth finger. Tears sting the backs of my eyes as a thick boulder of emotion lodges in my throat.

"What do you think?" Autumn asks.

I clear my throat and croak out, "It's perfect."

Cora stares at me in awe and sheer amazement. Then her eyes flick to Autumn. "Have time for me?" she asks.

"Yeah, sure. Just fill out the paperwork and give me a moment to sanitize the station."

Cora hops up and goes to the woman at the front. I amble behind her. "You don't need to get ink unless you want to, baby."

"I know. And I want to."

I nod and watch as she fills out the consent form and provides her license. Ten minutes later, we are back in the booth and Cora is sitting in the chair. Her shirt is hiked up and rests on her bra. Thankfully, the only skin exposed is what anyone would see if she were in a bathing suit. Otherwise, I might have hovered over her worse than a parent of a teenager.

"You ready?" Autumn asks Cora.

She nods and takes my hand. When Autumn presses the pedal and the gun starts buzzing, Cora jumps a little. I draw circles with my thumb over her hand and try to soothe her nervousness. "It only hurts for a minute. Then it numbs a little from the vibration."

The gun draws black lines on her skin just below her left breast. I sit mesmerized as Cora gets her first tattoo. It isn't just the fact that this is her first tattoo, but what she decided to imprint her skin with. Autumn dips the gun in the ink then comes back to Cora's ribcage.

When Autumn swipes some of the excess ink off, I

squeeze Cora's hand a little tighter. Cora peeks up at me, her smile brighter than the sunrise this morning.

"You okay?" she asks.

"I didn't think this day could get any better. But I was definitely wrong."

"Wait until you see what I do next." Cora giggles.

Wait, what? Is she getting another tattoo? Maybe she means something completely unrelated. Something when we leave here.

Another ten minutes pass before the tattoo gun is set down and Autumn is cleaning the tattoo and covering it up. Just beneath Cora's left breast rests my name in a feminine font. I am completely awestruck. It was one thing for me to get her name permanently etched into my skin, but I never expected her to reciprocate.

As I stand dazed, Cora asks me to go to the waiting area. For a moment, I am confused and ask her why.

"It's a surprise. Please," she pleads.

I nod and walk out to the waiting area, plop down onto the couch and grab a magazine. Every time I hear Autumn's tattoo gun spark to life, I peer toward the back of the studio. All I see is Autumn's head hunched over Cora.

What is she getting now?

Forever passes and I haven't heard the tattoo gun spark up in minutes. I toss the magazine to the table and rise from the couch. After I wear a new pattern into the linoleum floor, Cora walks back out to the waiting area. I pay and we walk out the door. The walk to the car is silent and I am dying more than ever to know what else she had done.

Once we are in the car, I ask, "So, what else did you get?" For whatever reason, I am more antsy now than I was when I asked Cora to marry me.

Cora faces me and juts her left hand toward me. On her ring finger, where her engagement ring sat less than twenty minutes ago, is a black band of ink that matches mine. It is slightly thinner, but otherwise mirrors mine. "Baby…" I whisper. "You didn't need to do that. I got you rings."

She nods and smiles. "I know, but I want the world to know I belong to you. No one else. Always." Cora throws my sentiment from earlier back at me. It steals my breath and kick-starts my pulse. Thank god we are in the confines of her car, otherwise I may have hit the ground. When I glance down at her right hand, I notice she has moved her engagement ring to that side. She takes stock of where my eyes focus and answers before I ask. "I'm only wearing it on my right while it heals. Promise."

The fact that she worries if it bothers me her engagement ring sits on her right hand is adorable. Honestly, which hand her ring is on is the furthest thing from my mind. Right now, I want to take her home and make love to her until our bodies give out. Celebrate that we are finally getting the happily ever after we deserve after so many years apart.

Today, Cora permanently gave herself to me as I have her. With each passing second, the day gets better and better.

I nod. "Let's go home, baby. I'm dying to make love to my fiancée."

November 21 - Seven months later

"Come on, Cora. You do *not* want to be late today," Shelly yells from the living room.

"I'll be out in a second," I yell back at her. I scan the room, checking every surface to make sure I haven't forgotten anything. Satisfied, I grab the two bags on my bed then turn and walk out of the bedroom.

When I enter the living room, I glimpse my best friend who is currently trying to wear a new pattern into the wood floor with her heels. She mumbles under her breath, but stops when she spots me.

"Did you feed Luna?" I ask.

"Yes. Everything is done. You ready to go?"

I glance down and inventory the bags in my hands.

"Ready," I answer. "Erin picked up the other totes and food already?"

"Yeah, she left a few minutes ago."

I nod. Shelly and I grab our purses, I give Luna one last pat and kiss, then we head out the door. We deposit the bags in her back seat and jump in the front. Seconds later, we are on the road and driving toward Sand Key park.

I stare out the window, take in the blue skies, fluffy white clouds, and sparkling sunlight, then thank the weather gods for keeping everything perfect today.

The weather has turned cool, but it isn't cold yet. Thanksgiving is right around the corner and this year I am thankful more than any year prior. For destiny and Gavin and the best circle of friends a person could ask for. Too often, we take life and the people we see daily for granted. After losing Gavin and getting him back, I take nothing for granted. Each day, I thank my lucky stars life brought us back together.

Over the last seven months, the emotional scale of our friends was all over the place. One day they loved us. The next, they freaked out. Shelly questioned me for hours once I flaunted my engagement ring. She had seen all my tears. All of them. She experienced my pain. Both times. And she wanted to be sure I wasn't acting on a whim. That I hadn't said yes because I felt pressured by the question or situation.

Everyone thought the engagement and us getting

married was too soon. Irrational and foolish. That we should wait. Give it a year or so. Especially after rekindling what we once lost. Spend more time learning the adult versions of each other.

"You can't rely on your feelings from the past, Cora." Shelly had said. And I don't.

What I felt for Gavin in our early teen years is nothing compared to what I feel for him now. Circumstances ripped us apart. Tested our strength and ability to love. Time had been our enemy, but also our saving grace. Without time apart, Gavin and I may have become complacent in our relationship. Grown apart. But time hardened us. Made us see the world and life and love in a different light.

When we each hit a point in our lives of numbness, of not caring about anything aside from daily monotony, fate brought us back together. Showed us how life could be if we gave us another chance. The short road was rocky, but our hearts knew from day one.

Hints of skepticism floated in the air from our friends, but every time they saw us attached at the hip with rosy eyes, their doubts were squandered.

Now when I look at my friends, all I see was happiness. For me. For Gavin. And for what we have together.

In no time, we drive into the park and weave around the outskirts. Shelly drives to the designated location, not far from the beach parking, and parks the car.

Soon, we have all the bags out of the car and in the

makeshift dressing room. Shelly attacks me with makeup brushes as soon as my butt hits the chair. I close my eyes and let her do her magic while I go to my happy place—Gavin. As Shelly swipes a soft-bristled brush over my cheek, Erin walks into the tent.

"Hey, ladies. How's it going in here?"

Erin is dressed in a knee-length bloodred lacy dress with a nude underlay. Her curly red locks are pinned up in a loose chignon while a few long strands frame her face. Her makeup is subtle and accentuates her freckled skin. Shelly has her hair pinned in the same fashion. And soon, Shelly will don the same dress when she finishes my makeup. Seeing my best friends like this is surreal. For the longest time, I never thought a day like today would be in my future.

"We are on schedule. How's everything else?" Shelly asks Erin.

Erin gives two thumbs up. "All according to plan." Before I can ask what *according to plan* entails, Erin sneaks out of the tent and leaves.

Shelly continues the task at hand. I follow her hands with my eyes and wish there was a mirror nearby for me to catch a glimpse. Considering I barely wear makeup in the first place, it seems as if she put every product from Ulta on my face. As if she reads my mind, she meets my gaze and smiles.

"You don't need to worry about anything. Today will

be perfect. Take a deep breath and let everything happen how it's meant to."

I nod, close my eyes again, and let her work her magic.

One breath in. One breath out.

GAVIN

Standing on the semi-warm sand, I wriggle my toes through the soft grains as I peer over my shoulder at the closed-off tent.

Shelly's car is parked just outside the tent, so I know my girl is inside. What are they doing inside that small tent? Can't be much based on the size. And how much longer will I have to wait to see her? I check my watch. Thirty minutes. Only thirty more minutes and she will stand beside me.

I stroll farther down the beach and out of the view of the tent. Popping my earbuds in, I crank up my music and stare out at the water. Feels like it has taken us a century to reach this exact moment, but the day has finally arrived. Finally.

Fifteen years ago today, my best friend became something greater than I could fathom at the time. Something bigger than my fourteen-year-old brain could comprehend or imagine. She became the love of my life.

Honestly, she had been since day one, but I wasn't equipped to understand such things.

If we had been together the whole time, no doubt married before now, we would celebrate our fifteenth anniversary today. But rather than celebrate this day as boyfriend and girlfriend—an antiquated term—today, we will officially become husband and wife.

Cora will be my wife. Mine. Forever.

The second everyone found out we were engaged, the first question that popped up was "Have you set a date?" We hadn't discussed dates, but, funny enough, we both blurted out November 21 at the same time. It was our day. Always will be. Until death do us part, and beyond.

Someone taps my shoulder and I turn to see Mom as I take an earbud out. "Hey, sweetie. You should probably get in position. Things will start soon."

I nod. "Thanks, Mom. Love you." I kiss her cheek.

She kisses the air next to my cheek, careful to not smear her lipstick on me. "Love you, too." After a quick hug, she walks off and joins everyone else not in the tent.

I wander toward the makeshift aisle, arch, and chairs. Cora and I are far from traditional. But our style resonates in every flower arrangement, decor piece, and article of clothing we all wear today. We kept the number of attendees to a minimum—twenty people, including Cora's maid of honor and my best man. On the aisle side of each row of chairs is a small bundle of black calla lilies and red roses—identical flowers to Cora's bouquet and the boutonnière flowers. Although Erin isn't in the wedding party, we got her an identical dress to Shelly since she is taking photos for and with us.

The arch at the end of the aisle is decorated in black and red sheer fabrics and flowers. Cora's mother and Shelly did an awesome job with the floral arrangements. They truly scream us and our style. As does our ensemble for the day. Although I have yet to see her dress, Cora and I are both in black. While Shelly and Micah are in red.

I slip my earbuds in their case and set them, and my phone, with my other clothes.

Before I grasp the gravity of it all, I walk down the aisle, bare feet crunching in the sand and heart jackhammering in my chest. When I reach the arch, I spin and stand in my place. Hands clasped at the front of my waist.

Micah walks up and stands beside me and pats my shoulder. "You nervous, bro?"

I stare down the aisle and shake my head. "I've been waiting for this day my entire life. Just can't wait to call her my wife." Those words hold so much truth.

As soon as the words leave my lips, the music starts. "Back In Black" by AC/DC blares from the setup speakers and echoes off the water. This song has nothing to do with weddings or love, but is one-hundred-percent us.

Gavin and Cora.

And the best fucking song to replace the traditional wedding march.

My breath comes in sharp bursts as I fumble with my fingers, eager to see her. One, two, three heartbeats later, Cora steps around a sand dune and I stop breathing. Dress black as night, several layers of tulle ghost the sand as she grips her father's elbow and walks toward me. The V-line bust of her dress is vintage lace that comes to a point at her solar plexus and also decorates the length of her arms. And just below the hollow of her throat is the locket her mother gave her years ago. A locket that now holds pictures of us.

"Fuck, she is gorgeous," I mutter and a couple people laugh. But I give no fucks. Cora is absolutely stunning and I refuse to take my eyes off her.

That is my wife. Mrs. Cora Elizabeth Hunt. My best friend. My lover. My life.

CORA

I round the sand dune with Dad on my arm, catch sight of Gavin near the arch, and suck in a breath.

Goddamn. I am one lucky-ass woman.

Gavin stands clad in a long-sleeve black button-down, the top two buttons undone, and black dress slacks. His red rose and black calla lily boutonnière rests above his left breast pocket. A thin layer of stubble accentuates his jawline as his hair kicks up with the occasional breeze. And the second he sees me, he bounces a little in place.

At the end of the aisle, Dad clings to my arm and gives me a quick squeeze. "Ready, pumpkin?"

I peek up at him for a split second, then revert my eyes back to my husband—*husband*—twenty feet away. Am I ready? I have been ready for this moment for as long as I can remember. "Yeah, Daddy. I've been ready."

We both take a deep breath, then Dad slowly guides me down the aisle and closer to Gavin. The love of my life. The man I don't ever wish to live a day without. The other half of my soul.

When we reach Gavin, Dad gives me a kiss on the cheek, unhooks his arm from mine, and goes to sit next to Mom.

Gavin and I lock eyes and the world around us disappears. The only other person in our bubble is the ordained minister. He begins speaking the preplanned speech, but neither of us hears a word of it. We are both well aware we don't have lines to speak for at least another minute. Until then, we drink each other in. Bask in the love we share.

I love you, Gavin mouths.

I love you too, I mouth back.

"Gavin and Cora have prepared their own vows and

will read them to each other now. Gavin…" the minister says.

Gavin takes a deep, shuddering breath and keeps his gaze locked on mine. "Cora… We have overcome so many obstacles to get to where we are right now. And I'm so glad we did. All that aside, I remember the first day I fell in love with you. The first day of freshman year. Yeah, we were barely friends that day, but one look at you and I knew you were the one. Under that shady oak tree, our tree, everything changed. And afterward, in art, when I caught you drawing me into a self-portrait, I fell even harder."

The backs of my eyes burn. Tears threatening to break free. My throat closes in on itself as emotion chokes me. My fingers wring the stems of the bouquet as I hold his gaze.

"Months later, on this very day, we became more than friends. We became each other's everything. Every single damn day, I am thankful for you. For the love you give me. To have you at my side. To have you in my life. More than anything, I am thankful you gave me your heart and love in return. I've already experienced life without you, and know that will never happen again. Cora Elizabeth Davies, I give you me. All of me. The good, the bad and all the parts in between. I want to experience every day, for the rest of our lives, with you by my side. Forever."

He plucks the matching wedding band for my

engagement ring from his pocket and slips it on my finger, resting it atop the tattoo that matches his own, then slides my engagement band on after. I stare down at our hands and breathe easier than I ever have. Everything about this moment, about Gavin and I joining our lives in every possible way, feels more right than anything.

Feels more at home than ever before.

Gavin finishes his vows and I swap my bouquet with Shelly for a tissue. I dab my eyes and take a deep breath. "Cora..." the minister says.

GAVIN

Cora slips her hands into mine and her fingers tremble beneath mine. Her eyes stained red from the happy tears she cried while I said my vows and slipped her wedding band on her finger. She peeks skyward and bats her lashes a few times before bringing her eyes back to mine. Then she smiles and my heart gallops in my chest.

"Gavin..." My name is a prayer on her lips. "You have brought so much into my life. Laughter and love, strength and beauty. Together, we have been through so much. Time may have been stolen from us, but you can't shake destiny. And that's what you are—my fate. My destiny. Fifteen years ago, you became something greater than my best friend. You became my everything. My first boyfriend. My first real kiss. And some things we won't discuss in front of company."

I burst out in laughter and our audience mimics.

"From that fateful first day during freshman year, the one where you sat beside me and ate the nasty school casserole, I knew we would never only be friends. But friends was the perfect place for us to start. Because through our friendship, we fell madly and deeply in love with each other. Gavin, I never want to experience another day of our lives apart. How can I not believe in kismet when it brought you to me more than once? Gavin Eli Hunt—see, even our parents knew we were two halves of a whole and gave us similar middle names. Life without you isn't one worth living and I am eager to see what the future holds for us. I love you beyond comprehension. Will love you until we both take our last breath. Always."

Cora takes my black titanium band in her nimble fingers and slides it up my ring finger. Nothing has felt as amazing as this moment right here. The moment we seal our lives together and become one. A unit.

My life is her life. And hers is mine. My fucking wife. *Fuck.*

The tears are coming and I am about to cry like a bitch. But I don't give a shit. This woman is in my blood. My heart. My every breath. And fuck if I don't want to kiss the hell out of her right now.

The minister starts talking and I work hard to listen.

Needless to say, it is a challenge. "Cora, do you take Gavin to be your lawfully wedded husband? Through good times and bad, sickness and health, until death do you part?"

Cora's smile brightens the setting sun. "Hell yes."

"That's my girl." I laugh.

"Gavin, do you take Cora to be your lawfully wedded wife? Through good times and bad, sickness and health, until death do you part?"

"Fuck yeah. And we're never dying, baby."

The crowd roars in laughter as the minister pronounces us husband and wife, and finally gives us permission to kiss. I wrap my *wife* in my arms and kiss the fuck out of her. In front of everyone, I kiss her like no one else exists.

Because no one does. And never will. It is just me and my girl. Forever. Always.

Five years later

"YOU ALRIGHT, BABY?" I ask Cora as we hit the three-mile marker of a five-mile trail in the redwood forest.

"I need a water break."

We stop on the trail and drink water for a minute. We have been hiking a little more than an hour, but we are more than halfway. Cora has been a trooper during this trip. Nonstop adventure. But we plan to only be in California for a couple weeks and I want to show her all the wonderful parts. The places I knew she would fall in love with.

California is definitely different than Florida with all its monster-sized trees and mountains. The scent of the air and saltiness of the water is different too. As much as

I miss the landscape and long list of adventures here, I love our little slice of Florida more.

For our five-year anniversary, Cora suggested we come out to California and visit Mom, but also share some adventures of our own. The redwoods, Yosemite, and some of the obvious tourist spots. Our trip so far has been incredible.

Currently, Mom is watching Clara, our three-year-old daughter. Us visiting California is more than a treat for Mom. Not only does she get to spend time with me and Cora, but she also gets to spoil Clara rotten.

Clara is the most amazing gift Cora has given me, aside from her heart. Until the day Cora told me we were pregnant, I never pictured myself as a father. Not that I didn't want to have children with Cora. More like I was so wrapped up in our bubble, I didn't envision beyond it.

But becoming a parent is one of the most awe-inspiring experiences. From learning we would soon be three instead of two to watching my gorgeous wife's belly grow to seeing my daughter enter the world. As a man, I saw the world one way. As a husband, I saw it another. Now, as a father, I see so much more. More love. More possibility. Just more.

"Ready to finish the back half of the trail?" I ask Cora.

"Ready as I'll ever be."

We continue along the rest of the trail, hand in hand. On occasion, we stop and admire something we see.

Plants and trees, animals and streams. Nature and wildlife in California are the polar opposite of Florida, and Cora is in seventh heaven. Being in the middle of the forest is one of her favorite things and, every opportunity we can, we adventure somewhere with forestry.

After we reach the end of the trail, we call Mom's house and talk with both her and Clara. Since we are in northern California, we won't be at Mom's tonight to tuck Clara in. Cora and I are staying at a bed-and-breakfast just outside of San Francisco and enjoying a couple days of our anniversary alone.

"Night, night, Daddy," Clara says. Her voice is the cutest thing I have ever heard in my life. The melody is a sweeter, younger extension of Cora. Part of me wonders if Cora sounded the same when she was Clara's age. Either way, it melts my heart and makes me goo in her little hands.

"Night, pumpkin," I say and make a kissing sound into the phone. "Be good for Nana. I love you and we'll see you tomorrow."

"Love you, Daddy."

"Here's Mommy."

I hand the phone to Cora and she and Clara have an in-depth conversation about which is better—chocolate chip cookies or brownies. Cora tells Clara her favorite is the brookie we buy at the vegan bakery near home. Cora yanks the phone away from her ear as Clara starts yelling "brookie" over and over. Clara and Cora

exchange goodnights and I love yous before discon-
necting the call.

"I really hope Mom isn't feeding her cookies and
brownies. We'll never be able to curb her cravings once
we leave," I say and wince.

"Yeah, I hope not either."

I drive us back to the bed-and-breakfast and we get
ready to go out for our anniversary date. As Cora puts
on her jeans and sweater, I notice the way she stares at
her outfit with extra scrutiny.

"Everything okay, baby?" I ask as I pull her into
a hug.

She snakes her arms around my waist and squeezes
me tight. "Everything's fine. Just wondering if I brought
warm enough clothes. The weather here is so much
different than home."

"You look beautiful," I admit. "And if you get cold,
just say the word and I'll keep you warm." I kiss the top
of her head.

Once dressed and ready, we head to the restaurant in
the city. Since Cora loves everything Asian, I thought she
would love tasting how amazing food is out here. We
arrive at the restaurant and are seated right away. After
we order drinks, I notice Cora didn't get a glass of wine
—her typical choice when we go out and don't have to
worry about Clara.

Cora plays with her napkin and then places it in her
lap. She stares at her lap a minute before locking her

gaze with mine. Teeth capture her bottom lip and worry it.

"Baby, you sure everything is okay? You're worrying me."

She releases her lip. A smile brightens her face as she holds my gaze. "We're pregnant." And just like that, her confession steals my breath.

CORA

"Gavin? Did I break you?"

A minute ago, I told Gavin we were pregnant. Again. I expected his response to be like last time. Screams and cheers and swinging me in the air. Instead, he just sits across from me, frozen. A few minutes ago, he said he was worried. Now it seems to be my turn to worry.

Does he not want more children now?

It's not as if we have done much in the prevention department. We have actually been pretty up-front about children and our future. Especially after we learned I was pregnant with Clara. Since I don't have much time left to safely carry a baby, we thought trying now for a second baby was better than waiting.

But now, his current state has me not so sure.

Finally, his face relaxes. "You took a test?"

"Yeah, a couple days ago, after a trip to the store with your mom. She doesn't know, though."

"Why didn't you tell me you thought you were pregnant? I hate that you were wondering alone."

I didn't have a logical explanation as to why I hadn't told him yet. Guess I just wanted to give it another day or two before I took a test. Plus, we were going on our trip.

"Sorry I didn't let you know I suspected it. I'll blame it on foggy, pregnancy brain. You're not upset, are you?"

Gavin shakes his head. "No, baby, I'm not upset. The opposite actually. I just wish I could've waited for the positive result next to you. I know it's way too early to know, but I hope Clara gets a little brother."

I roll my eyes and he laughs. "I'm sure Clara will love him or her, no matter what gender they are. You sure you're okay, daddy?" Heat pierces Gavin's eyes and I swallow. The same heat that pops up every time I call him daddy… in my seductress voice.

"You don't need to worry about daddy, baby," he growls across the table. "But let's take the rest of the trip easy. Had I known before today, I wouldn't have taken us on a five-mile hike in the mountains."

"I'm not that fragile, Gavin. Besides, I need to maintain my girlish figure for as long as possible. Soon enough, I'll look like a whale."

Gavin shakes his head. "No, baby. You'll be the most beautiful woman in the world, still. There is nothing sexier than the love of my life carrying my unborn child inside her belly. If anything, you get sexier with each stretch mark."

Heat rises to my cheeks. "Gavin…" I whisper.

Dinner goes by much quicker after the *we're pregnant* conversation. Chinese food in San Francisco is phenomenal. Anytime we eat Asian in Florida now, I will undoubtedly whine and complain. Plus, I think pregnancy makes it taste even better.

We arrive back at the bed-and-breakfast and head to our room. Three breaths after the door closes, Gavin and I frantically rip each other's clothes off. In the last five years, a few things have changed in our relationship.

The addition of Clara.

Our need to kiss and grope and be completely consumed by each other.

How much we love each other.

The last two have multiplied to levels I never knew existed. With each passing day, I don't think I can possibly desire or love Gavin more than I already do. But each day I wake up next to him, his warm skin and beachy-pine wrapped around me, I learn a new truth.

Our love is boundless.

Gavin yanks my shirt over my head and tosses it to the floor before bruising my lips with his. The rest of our clothes hit the floor seconds before we land on the mattress. Everything about us—our life, our love—grows hotter with each passing day. As Gavin kisses down my body, he stops and hovers above my abdomen a moment.

"Hey, little man. Yeah, Daddy is predicting you'll be a boy. Don't let me down, okay? Us guys got to stick together." I laugh and Gavin continues. "Anyway, I can't wait to meet you. And for you to meet me and Mommy and Clara, your big sister." Gavin presses his lips to my belly and kisses me tenderly.

Gavin Hunt. My best friend. My lover. The best husband. And an even better father.

"I love you, Gavin," I whisper.

He crawls up my body and kisses me reverently. "I love you, too, baby. Forever."

"Always."

Bonus Content

Want more Gavin and Cora?
You can get their bonus story by going to
www.persephoneautumn.com/bonus-content

Thank You!

Thank you so much for reading **Time Exposure**, book two in the **Click Duet**. If you would take a moment to leave a review on the retailer site where you made your purchase, Goodreads and/or BookBub, it would mean the world to me.

Reviews help other readers find and enjoy the book as well.

Much love,
Persephone

Up Next in the Series

When I started the Click Duet, it wasn't my intention to write an entire duet series. But I connected and fell in love with this circle of friends. Glimpses of their stories popped into my head and I just knew there'd be more.

The Inked Duet—Fine Line (book one) and Love Buzz (book two)—are the next two installments in the Bay Area Duet Series.

Who's story is up next? Jonas and Autumn!

When Jonas lost his chance with Cora, I just knew his story would be next. And let me tell you, I love it so much and know you will too.

Second chance at love, single parent, a bit angsty, and dashes of suspense 🖤

Start reading Fine Line and Love Buzz now!

Click Duet Playlist

Here are some of the songs from the *Click Duet* playlist.
You can listen to the entire playlist on Spotify!

I Still Wait For You - XYLØ
Malibu Nights - LANY
i love you - Billie Eilish
High School Sweethearts - Melanie Martinez
The Beach - The Neighbourhood
Falling - Harry Styles
Out Of Love - Alessia Cara
BLUE - Troye Sivan, Alex Hope

More by Persephone Autumn

The Inked Duet

A man with a broken heart and a woman scared to put herself out there. Love is never easy. Sometimes love rips you apart. Fine Line (Inked Duet #1) and Love Buzz (Inked Duet #2) is a second chance at love, single parent romance with a pinch of angst and dash of suspense.

The Insomniac Duet

He was her high school bully. She was the outcast that secretly crushed on him. More than ten years later, he's her boss, completely oblivious to their shared past, and wants no one but her. More importantly, he doesn't understand her animosity toward him.

Transcendental

A musician in search of his muse and a woman grieving the loss of her husband. Two weeks at an exclusive retreat and their connection rivals all others. Until she leaves early without notice. But he refuses to give up until he finds her again.

Depths Awakened

A small town romance which captivates you from the start. Two broken souls have sworn off love. Vowed to never lose anyone else. But their undeniable attraction brings them together and refuses to let go.

Distorted Devotion
Swept off her feet by love, life takes a dark, unexpected turn. Now the love of her life may be the cause of her death. Check out this gripping, romantic suspense.

Undying Devotion
A long-term couple with a secret life. Their friends envy the bond they share, but remain oblivious to their lifestyle and how deep the bond lies. A turn of events has her wanting to spill every secret.

Beloved Devotion
She asks the love of her life to marry her. When her girlfriend hesitates, then says yes, she is determined to learn why. As the pieces start to fall in place, she discovers she doesn't know her fiancée at all.

Ink Veins
Persephone Autumn's debut collection, Ink Veins, explores topics of depression, love, and self-discovery with a raw, unfiltered voice.

<u>Broken Metronome</u>

When the music of the heart dies…

Broken Metronome is an angsty poetry collection full of heartache and the possibility of what may have been.

Connect with Persephone

Connect with Persephone

www.persephoneautumn.com

Subscribe to Persephone's Newsletter

www.persephoneautumn.com / newsletter

Join Persephone's Reader Group

Persephone's Playground

Follow Persephone Online

instagram.com / persephoneautumn

facebook.com / persephoneautumnwrites

goodreads.com / persephoneautumn

bookbub.com / authors / persephone-autumn

amazon.com / author / persephoneautumn

pinterest.com / persephoneautumn

twitter.com / PersephoneAutum

Acknowledgments

First up… my family!

Thank you for always cheering me on. For standing in my corner and supporting this journey in my life.

To my wife… for always being one of my biggest fans. For reading my books (when you get a break in your work schedule) and helping me brainstorm ideas. Also, you pimp me hardcore. Ask everyone you meet if they read books and then market like I pay you. Love you!

To my daughter… when I hit it big, you *will* be my social media guru. You're also one of my biggest fans 🖤 I wouldn't be as inspired if you hadn't entered my life. I am so proud to be your mom. Love you bunches!

To my dad… thank you for supporting my endeavors, boosting me when I need it, and being the best dad a woman could have. I wouldn't be the woman I am today without you. Love you more than words!

To Ellie and Rosa at My Brother's Editor… thank you for always correcting my commas, em dashes, words that I think should be one, words that should be one but I think are two, polishing my manuscript, hinting more detail, letting me know I used the same word a million times, and giving the best feedback. You ladies work so hard and I am proud to have you on my team. All the love to you both! xoxo

To Kat Savage… I want to take a road trip just to hug you! Thank you for creating gorgeous covers for my books. Thank you for enduring my random emails and texts. Thanks for putting up with my annoying ass when I can't decide on what I want 😄 Thanks for all you do (especially writing awesome books). You constantly inspire me to be better.

To all the kick ass peeps in Persephone's Playground… no words will ever be enough to express my gratitude. The fact that you love my words enough to join the reader's group… I am eternally grateful and humbled every day. I love you all!

To the ARC and promo team… author life is bananas! But you all make it easier. Thank you for reading my books before release day and sharing your feedback and reviews. Thank you for promoting my stories with your followers and friends. Without you, I'd be lost and crying in the corner.

To my incredible author friends… you know as much as I do that no set of words strung together will ever express the gratitude we have for the help we give each other. Thank you to the moon and back for being a part of this journey, reading my words, lending an ear (or screen), and sharing my cover reveals and releases. Having you in my world is the best gift. Kat Savage, Dee Lagasse, Mel Walker, Abigail Davies, Melissa Ryann, Christina Hart, J.R. Rogue, Elle Thorpe, Ellie Isaacson, JA Stone, T.K. Cherry, Q.B. Tyler, Andi Burns, and the mile long list of authors in the Inkers group. I love you all and am thankful to have you in my life!

To Patricia… thank you for creating the most wonderful book trailers for this duet! You've been on my team since the beginning. I am so appreciative for your awesome reviews and beautiful posts. So glad to have you on my team! xoxo

To Shelly… without fail, you support me daily. Thank you for being an incredible human! Wish I could drive up north and hug the heck out of you! Thank you for everything you do. I appreciate it more than you know. ALL THE GIFS FOR YOU!! xoxo

To every person you picked up this book and read it… thank you from the bottom of my heart. Having someone choose to read your words is an author dream come true. And I wouldn't be where I am without readers. I am beyond humble that anyone wants to read the stories in my head. Thank you will never be enough. So much gratitude and love for each and every one of you! xoxo

About the Author

Persephone Autumn lives in Florida with her wife, crazy dog, and two lover-boy cats. A proud mom with a cuckoo grandpup. An ethnic food enthusiast who has fun discovering ways to veganize her favorite non-vegan foods. If given the opportunity, she would intentionally get lost in nature.

For years, Persephone did some form of writing; mostly journaling or poetry. After pairing her poetry with images and posting them online, she began the journey of writing her first novel.

She mainly writes romance, but on occasion dips her toes in other works. Look for her poetry publications and a psychological horror under P. Autumn.